"To my
Luv U° —Serena°

de

❀

A YEAR OF
PINK ROSES

A YEAR OF PINK ROSES

A Novel

Siu Fai Li

iUniverse, Inc.
New York Lincoln Shanghai

A Year of Pink Roses

iUniverse books may be ordered through booksellers or by contacting:

iUniverse
2021 Pine Lake Road, Suite 100
Lincoln, NE 68512
www.iuniverse.com
1-800-Authors (1-800-288-4677)

This is a work of fiction. All of the characters, names, incidents, organizations, and dialogue in this novel are either the products of the author's imagination or are used fictitiously.

ISBN-13: 978-0-595-42401-6 (pbk)
ISBN-13: 978-0-595-86738-7 (ebk)
ISBN-10: 0-595-42401-5 (pbk)
ISBN-10: 0-595-86738-3 (ebk)

Printed in the United States of America

Sometimes love comes so easily, sometimes love is a constant struggle, and there are times when we go from one extreme to the other, speeding dizzily along, never knowing how everything changed so suddenly, never knowing how we got there.

It was a sunny autumn day in the city. There was a refreshing bit of chill in the air, and the leaves were just starting to display the colors which heralded the change into winter. It was a lovely time of the year, everything seemed so brisk and alive. It was a nice time to be outdoors; to feel the wind on your cheeks, to watch the sunlight dancing across the leaves, to wander amidst the faces in the streets. It was a good time to be living.

The train was slowly making its way downtown when James saw Lauren for the first time. Even through the hazy window of the subway, he noticed the beautiful woman standing on the platform as the train rolled by her. She entered the subway car and took a seat opposite his. Their eyes met briefly and they greeted each other with a soft, silent smile. James' mind raced and his heart leapt for a moment. His thoughts traveled quickly; he imagined the two of them falling in love, waltzing blissfully at their wedding, enjoying everyday of their wonderful life together, and sailing through their golden years as much in love as ever. A silent euphoria enveloped James in his fantasy, bringing an unseen smile to his lips. It would be nice, he thought.

James was riding the subway down to West Village, a small section of the city where streets were still cobblestoned and sidewalks were scattered with outdoor cafes. It was a nice neighborhood for a leisurely stroll. The area had more than its share of art galleries, music, and restaurants that were decidedly a change of pace from the usual day-to-day fare. It also featured an eclectic menagerie of faces and bodies flowing through its streets, drawn by the offbeat culture. It was a popular section of the city, a paradox of trendy boutiques and weathered cafes in a timeworn neighborhood. It was also just a nice place to be.

The train jerked its way out of the station and continued its journey downtown. James looked around at his fellow passengers. He was not the only one who noticed the beautiful woman sharing his train. He wondered if she were in their thoughts as well. It was amazing, James thought, the power of beauty, what a strong, profound effect it had on people. His mind began to drift again. In appearances, he thought, they were not a match. She was incredibly beautiful, someone who turned heads in a crowded room, while he was somewhat average, someone who would go unnoticed. What would people say?

James was awakened from his reverie as the train stopped at the next station. A large group of people poured into the train and quickly filled the remaining seats, those who were slow of feet were left to stand in the aisles. Unfortunately, a small crowd filled the space between the beautiful woman and James, and he was sadly separated from his would-be partner in life. He took his bad luck begrudgingly and was even pouting a little when he noticed an older woman standing, holding onto the subway car with small, frail hands. James waved to her and offered her his seat. She graciously made her way toward him and rewarded him with a soft "thank you" as she settled into the chair. James smiled at her. It was nothing. He forgot about the beautiful woman across the aisle.

The train was crowded, but before long it reached his stop. He left the subway and slowly made his way up toward sunlight. It was a little past noon, as good a time as any for lunch. There was a small cafe in the neighborhood that James liked. It was nestled in a quiet side-street and served good, inexpensive vegetarian fare. On sunny days, the cafe put a few tables outside so that people could sit in the fresh air and enjoy the beautiful weather. The restaurant was a few blocks' walk from the station, and James strolled leisurely in the autumn air. The sun beamed through the mild chill and warmed him as he made his way through the streets. The sunny weather had drawn many people outdoors that day. The streets were busy and bustling, everyone with their particular destinations.

The cafe was a pleasant sight as James walked down the cobblestoned street. It was familiar and comforting. There was a small crowd waiting outside. He would have to wait for a small while, he thought. The tables outside were all filled with people, happily sipping their coffees, eating their sandwiches, picking at their salads, all intent on lazily enjoying their small privileged place in the sun.

James took his place in line and waited. There was only one party ahead of him. They looked like students from the nearby college. There was no hurry that day; it was too beautiful a day to rush. As he turned to watch the pedestrian traffic passing by, James caught a glimpse of someone familiar walking toward the cafe. It was the woman from the train. A smile rose within him at the sight. It was good to see her again, he thought, as if she were a long-lost friend. The warm feelings seemed misplaced since, after all, they didn't even know each other; but the excitement was there all the same.

She cast her eyes toward James as she reached the cafe, then she turned into the entrance and walked toward him.

"We meet again," she smiled as she approached James. It was a beautiful smile, the kind of smile which made you forget who you were, where you were, what you were doing. It offered an exuberance of warmth and comfort that wrapped itself around you and held you in its delicate embrace. And that wonderful smile was meant for him!

It was a scene out of a dream. James imagined that he had been waiting for this moment for an eternity. It seemed that time had stopped at this pivotal moment, waiting for him to act, waiting for him to respond. James always thought that if he knew what to say, what to do at such a moment, everything would fall into place from that point in time. If only he had the right words.

"Hello again," James smiled back at her, "I guess I was followed." She laughed. There was a twinkle in her eyes as she laughed. It was soft, earnest, and feminine. It seemed to James to be the most wonderful sound in the world.

"This is one of my favorite restaurants," she said, "do you come here often?"

James had to admit to her that he did not. He wished that he did; it would have been something in common that they would have shared. They could discuss their favorite moments there, favorite meals, favorite wines. Maybe they would have met previously, exchanging glances from separate tables. Maybe they could have fallen in love …

James began to chat with her as they waited outside the restaurant. They talked mostly about the food; the always good vege burgers, the yummy soba noodles, and the brown rice stir fry that was sometimes good, sometimes so-so. James thought how nice it was just talking with her. A day that was already so beautiful was made infinitely more brilliant. He secretly wished that they would have a long wait for their table, so that he could continue talking to her. Despite his silent prayer, a couple that was seated at an outside table got up to leave, and the college students decided to settle into a large table inside the restaurant.

The hostess approached James and asked if he would like the outside table. He halfheartedly assented, hesitant to leave the beautiful stranger. "Give me a minute, and I'll have the table ready for you guys in a second," the hostess answered. Oh, we're not together, he wanted to explain, but the words caught in his throat. The hostess turned away from them and went to clean off the table left vacant by the couple. James turned to his new friend, not knowing exactly what to say, what to do. Before he could think of something to say, she laughed softly and said, "I guess we're sharing a table. You don't mind, do you?"

The hostess returned with two menus and asked them to follow her. They turned toward each other with a knowing smile, delighting in the secret (they weren't together!) that only the two of them shared. They settled into the small metallic table sitting in a sunny spot outside the cafe. The hostess told them that the waitress would soon be with them, and left to resume her position at the cafe entrance.

They were alone, and James really didn't know what to do next. He was nervous, nervous with the novelty of the situation, nervous with anticipation, nervous with doubts of what was to come. She sensed his anxiety, he thought, and she tried to put him at ease. She held out her hand to him.

"Hi, I'm Lauren", she said.

James shook her hand gratefully. "James. Nice to meet you," he answered.

She smiled at him again. "That was really nice of you on the train," she continued, "I don't see many people doing that anymore, you know, giving up their seats. I was going to give her my seat, but you beat me to it."

It was a minor good deed which James performed regularly, but this was the first time anyone commended him on it. "Thanks, it was nothing," he answered.

There was a pause in the conversation. James yearned to break the silence with a flood of questions about the beautiful woman with whom he shared the small table. She seemed mysterious, yet warm and familiar. He wondered who she was, what she did, why she was having lunch with him. His thoughts were interrupted by a waitress who approached their table. She introduced herself as Mimi and proceeded to ask them for their drink orders. Lauren ordered a Chardonnay and James asked for a Coke. The waitress repeated the lunch specialties and then left for the drinks. They were alone again.

"So, James, tell me about yourself," Lauren asked.

James honestly did not know what to say. It seemed an easy question, but it was hard to know where to begin. James moved to the city a long time ago and pretty much grew up here. He went to college in Philadelphia … The conversation seemed scripted, but it was born out of spontaneous interest. She wanted to know about his past, where he had been, what he had done. Lauren slowly pieced James' life together, which was more interesting to her than it was to him.

The waitress returned with the drinks and waited for their lunch orders. Neither James nor Lauren had looked at the menu or even thought about food just yet, so they each hastily ordered their favorites; a vege burger with sweet potato fries for her, and a soupy soba concoction for him.

"What do you do?" she asked.

James had always been hesitant about telling people that he was a doctor. He didn't want someone to like him or dislike him because of his profession. He wanted people to like him because of who he was.

"I work in an ER," he told her.

"Are you a doctor?" she asked with interest; James had to confess to her that he was.

"You almost seem embarrassed about it," she continued.

James told her that he didn't like the stereotype that came with the profession.

"I understand completely, I don't like telling people what I do, either," she said.

"What do you do?" he asked.

"I can tell you, but then I'll have to kill you," she replied with a smile.

It was an old joke, but it was unexpected, it was funny, and James laughed.

The waitress returned with their food. James smiled at the waitress as she served them, eager for her to leave so they could be alone again. He watched Lauren silently as he tasted his soba, paying little attention to the flavor of the noodles. He watched her take a bite of her burger. She puts ketchup on her burger and fries; he would have to remember that. They continued their conversation in between bites of their lunch, sometimes answering with a mouthful of "mmm hm" or an enthusiastic "ymm". It was not easy to eat soupy noodles and talk at the same time, especially since James had a tendency of slurping. When he slipped and slurped up a long string of soba, he looked up embarrassingly from his bowl of noodles and saw that she was smiling softly at him. She swallowed her mouthful of food and pardoned him. "That's ok. I slurp my noodles too." James smiled apologetically. He was beginning to feel quite at ease with his lunch partner.

The table offered a good vantage point of the sidewalk traffic, and conversely, the passers-by had a good view of them as well. There were a lot of glances their way, or more accurately; there were a lot of glances her way. Lauren was very pretty, and she attracted a lot of attention, almost as if she were an ornament placed in front of the restaurant. James found it amusing watching all the heads turn from the corner of his eye. He wondered if she knew that she attracted so much attention. He always believed that beautiful people knew that they were beautiful. She must have known, he thought. Did she mind people staring at her, watching her, admiring her? Did she enjoy the attention, or was it unwelcome?

There was something special in being seen with a beautiful woman. It was not that she was an ornament, a trophy; but it was a feeling that somehow you felt yourself elevated in her presence. He felt more attractive, more secure, more alive simply from being with her. Perhaps it really wasn't so much that she was beautiful, but the mere fact that someone chose to spend her time with him. He was worthwhile to someone, and that simple fact made him feel better about himself.

James finished his soba before long, and Lauren was cleaning off the remnants of her sweet potato fries. James thought that even if this lunch were to be all the time that he would have with Lauren, it was still a wonderful, serendipitous, remarkable time in his life. It was nice to have a moment in the sun, so to speak.

They were still talking animatedly when the waitress returned to the table. She cleared the dishes and asked them if they wanted any coffee or dessert. James wanted the meal to last as long as possible, so he had already planned on having both, even though he seldom ordered dessert. He was happy when Lauren asked for a coffee, seemingly joining his effort to prolong their time together. The waitress turned her attention to James. "Make that two coffees," he answered, and asked for a slice of cheesecake, two forks, inviting Lauren to split the rich dessert with him.

Mimi returned quickly with their coffees and the cheesecake. They poured milk and sugar into the coffees and each took a sip before proceeding onto the dessert. Milk, one sugar; James repeated to himself, depositing another bit of Lauren into his memory. Lauren and James dug their forks into the smooth confection and tasted the satiny cheesecake, which was particularly good that day. "Yummy," Lauren beamed. James was delighted in her "yummy" since he was one of the few people he knew who said "yummy" all the time. They slowly shared the cheesecake, delighting in each other's happy facial expressions as they finished the yummy dessert.

They sat and slowly sipped their coffees after dessert. James felt deliciously warm inside. It might have been the sun, the cheesecake, or the coffee; but it was more likely because of Lauren. He felt happy.

Inevitably, the waitress returned with the check, signaling the impending end to the best lunch that James ever had. Over his objections, Lauren insisted on splitting the tab. She didn't think it would be fair for him to pay for her lunch since they had just met. He was a little saddened to be reminded that he was still only a casual acquaintance to her, and the thought dampened his hopes of being someone more substantial. Maybe she wasn't interested.

Perhaps she wouldn't be interested, but James had already fallen completely for Lauren, and he didn't want things to end right there. James was always very anxious asking women out. There were a lot of emotions involved. Beforehand, he was completely inundated with hope and fear; hope of what could be, fear of what would not be. Her response would invariably leave him either very happy or very sad. He was asking someone (usually someone he already knew well) to accept him or reject him as a potential love interest. Sadly, James was often turned down, and though the women always let him down gently ("I like you as a friend", "You'll be a great catch", etc.), it was difficult not to take the rejections personally. He always felt inadequate afterward; that he was not good enough. It was understandable to feel anxious about asking someone out after so many rejections, since experience had taught him that the question often led to hurt feelings.

It was difficult to overcome his sense of fear and dejection at the time. We had a wonderful time together, didn't we? He knew he had a great time, but what about her? Did she also enjoy their time together? She seemed to like his company, or was she simply being nice? Their conversation was easy and they got along beautifully, he thought. They could become great friends, but what if she didn't feel the same way?

James wanted to see her again; he was sure of that. And for a moment, his desire had overcome his anxiety.

"Would you like to have dinner together some time?" There was a slight tremor in his voice, barely reflecting the wave of nervous uncertainty welling up inside of him.

"Sure," she replied. "That sounds like fun." She smiled and jotted down her phone number. James gave her his number in return. They were to call each other and arrange to meet on Friday. They left the restaurant and walked down the street together until they parted their ways a few blocks from the cafe. James watched her saunter away. She turned back after a few steps and saw him still watching her. She smiled and waved goodbye, then continued on her way. He turned toward no particular direction and walked on. Until Friday.

Lauren thought bemusedly about James after they parted. Kind of cute, she thought. There was something innocent and honest in his manner that was rather charming. She had first noticed him on the train when their eyes met and they exchanged smiles. She often received smiles from men, and she thought no further of the brief exchange. She relaxed and leaned back in the seat, glad to be heading home after a busy morning of work.

She was dressed in a simple white tee and a pair of jeans. The soft cotton shirt felt familiar and warm against her skin. Lauren had spent the morning in a modeling session for a magazine, and she was glad to be back in her street-clothes. A faded denim jacket laid upon her lap; she had taken it off earlier in the warmth of the autumn sun. It worked out well that she had the rest of the afternoon to herself, she thought. The weather was nice; it would be pleasant running her errands out in the beautiful day. She could have lunch outside at her favorite cafe, get a little sun, watch people go by, maybe do a little reading.

The train became more crowded at the next station as Lauren watched the passengers enter the car. Men and women jostled each other as they poured into the car, rushing for the few remaining seats. The once-empty aisle quickly filled with bodies pressed against each other, all eager to reach their destinations. Through the small space afforded by the crowd standing in front of her, she saw him getting up from his seat. An elderly woman took his place and thanked him graciously. It was the man with whom she exchanged smiles earlier. She smiled inwardly, he was a nice guy. It made her feel good to see niceness in the world. It made her believe in people.

They got off at the same station. Lauren saw him get off the train ahead of her. He was a few steps in front of her, separated by other men and women making their way out of the station. The bright sunlight caught her eyes as she reached the top of the stairs leading out of the subway. She looked around the sidewalks, but she had lost sight of him. He was gone, and Lauren realized that she didn't even know why she had looked for him. There was something about him which interested her, perhaps. She picked up her steps and walked to the corner, turning down the street which was home to her favorite cafe. She had put him out of her mind when she saw him from the far end of the block, a gentle profile with a slight slouch, waiting at the cafe. It was a nice surprise to see him there. Her step quickened ever so slightly. A genuine, friendly smile greeted her when he saw her approaching. He was glad to see her, too.

It was a fun lunch. The minutes passed by quickly, filled with smiles and delightful laughter. Lauren hadn't laughed so wholeheartedly in a long time. She was glad that the lunch worked out well. It was a bit of a chance having lunch with James. After all, she really didn't know him at all; although in retrospect, it was not any worse than a blind date.

Lauren found James to be a little shy, but he was a pleasant lunch partner once she opened up the conversation. She could tell that she made him a little nervous at first. It was nice to see that he did not put up a false bravado, as other men were apt to do. It made him more genuine and honest, plus there was something attractive about his vulnerability. It made him all the more endearing. He was very polite and attentive as they talked over lunch. Lauren felt very comfortable in the simplicity of his words and his gestures. He was funny, honest, kind, sincere; seemingly encompassing all that was wanted, needed by her. She couldn't put her finger on one thing from which he drew her interest. Perhaps it was a little bit of everything.

Lauren turned over bits and pieces of the time they spent together in her mind. The subway, the hostess, the table, the soba, the coffee. Inevitably, she mused over a mental picture of the two of them together, perhaps as good friends, perhaps as a couple. We hit it off really well, she said to herself.

She was not surprised that James had asked her to dinner afterward. As a matter of fact, she had expected it, and had been thinking it over when they had their coffee. She would be interested in seeing him again, she had decided. He was nice. It was a sweet and unexpected encounter, and in a way, very romantic, she thought.

James was cute, in an unremarkable kind of way, she thought. He was different from the guys that she dated. Most people would describe James as somewhat plain. The truth was that James' features were unremarkable in almost every way. Except for his Asian heritage and the slight accent which marked his ethnicity, he was unlikely to stand out in any crowd. There were streaks of grey here and there in his dark head of hair, but he still looked younger than his thirty-five years of age.

Lauren was a beautiful woman, and because of her work as a model, she met a lot of people at the many engagements and parties to which she was invited. She garnered a lot of attention from the men, who seldom remembered that she was more than a model. She had dated casually here and there. Her boyfriends were generally very handsome, pretty boys, as some people say. It wasn't that she was only interested in looks. She had her pick of men, and it was natural that she would choose someone who had it all; the face, the body, the personality, the education, the career. She looked for them to be funny, athletic, and she dismissed those who had no direction in life or career. Some men thought they could make an impression on her by playing the role of the big spender, but Lauren was not impressed by money. She made a great living as a successful model, so she did not want for wealth. Besides, she was not an extravagant person. She was unimpressed by dates that spent money excessively; she frowned upon their recklessness.

James was ecstatic when Lauren agreed to go out to dinner with him. He was generally a very grounded person. James approached most everything with a calm and even temperament. He would look over the different angles in any situation before he would proceed with action or judgment. It wasn't that he was not passionate, but he was very reserved. There was passion in him, but he kept it restrained.

In love, however, James was the polar opposite. He always dove in head first whenever he met someone that he was interested in. James was always ahead of himself in his relationships. Once he met someone who drew his interest, he would fantasize about how wonderful it would be for the two of them to be a couple together; how wonderful it would be to him for them to be together. Sometimes it happened from the first glance, even before he spoke to her, like he did with Lauren on the train. She looked like she would be kind, and sweet, and caring. He would award such accolades to her even before he knew her. He was almost ready to marry her then.

The same feelings would continue when they were dating. He imagined the two of them traveling, having adventures together, enjoying long intimate nights, how he would propose, how she would cry at the proposal with tears of joy, and say yes, yes, yes to all that he offered.

Although in his heart James always leapt with abandon, his shy nature often restrained him from asking women out. There he was, fantasizing about living with her, loving with her, but yet he could not take that first step of asking her out.

Perhaps it was the fear of rejection, the pain of rejection, which kept James restrained. Most of the time, women politely declined when he asked them out on a date. For whatever reason, James did not elicit much interest from women in general. It wasn't that he was bad-looking, had a bad personality, or bad prospects. His friends always wondered why he never met that someone special. At times when he was alone, James often became introspective and wondered if there was something he was missing, or something he could change about himself. "Was there something wrong with me?" was the general theme of these sullen musings.

In some ways, James was looking for a Princess Charming. Someone beautiful, someone strong, someone gentle, who would love him, cherish him, and protect him. She was someone fantastic, someone above his sphere, someone unattainable. In his ideal, she was always wonderful, lovely, kind, beautiful, but not perfect. She was always flawed in some way, something minor, something adorable. Perhaps she was messy, perhaps she was a picky eater, perhaps she was not well-read. It was an essential part of his ideal. She was imperfect in some way, and he loved her not less for it.

He often said to his friends that he was looking for someone who loved him when he was at his worst. That was true love, he thought, when someone loved you despite yourself. It was easy for his friends to see that James himself was that type of person that he was looking for. He was always a true friend; loyal, compassionate, kind, someone who would always be there for you no matter what. It's too bad that he hasn't found that someone, they whispered softly, it's too bad.

James was always a little intimidated by women, especially beautiful women. It seemed to him that they were perfectly happy going on with their beautiful lives without him getting in the way. It seemed to him that they deserved to be with someone that was better looking, someone who had more money, was more athletic; someone better. Perhaps it was only a matter of self-esteem, he realized, but that did not make it any less daunting for him to approach a woman.

He thought how fortunate it was for him to have had lunch with Lauren that day. It seemed like everything was set up just so for them to be together; the beautiful autumn day, the woman on the train, the hostess at the cafe. It was the kind of stuff that he dreamt about, and it actually happened.

The stars were aligned perfectly. It never occurred to James to feel intimidated or to feel uneasy being with Lauren. Sure, he was nervous at first, but his shyness was quickly melted away by Lauren's easy-going charm. It was so easy to talk to her, to sit with her, and to be with her.

At the time, Lauren had been seeing Brian for a few months. She met him at a party for a charity fund-raiser that her modeling agency had co-sponsored. He was an attorney in a large media company which made a sizable contribution to the event. With a little effort, Brian was able to procure one of the much sought-after invitations to the party, "to hang out with the models".

Lauren went to the party with some of her friends from the agency. As was always the case at such parties, the models attracted most of the attention from the men attending the event. The other women who were there spent much of the time talking together, since the men were otherwise preoccupied. This unfortunate circumstance was ripe cause for jealousy and petty criticism, and the other women had a fairly fine time themselves sipping drinks as they pointed out all the perceived shortcomings of the models.

Even in a room full of beautiful women, Lauren attracted a lot of attention. Brian was drawn to her instantly the moment he set his eyes on her. She was talking with a couple of people from his firm at the time. Brian saw his opening and walked over to the small group and greeted his co-workers, a little too warmly, then took his opportunity and introduced himself to Lauren.

At first, Lauren paid little attention to him, he was just another face in a room full of strangers. Brian, however, had made up his mind to attract Lauren's attention, and was constantly jumping into her conversation with his co-workers. Brian's words were well-rehearsed as he craftily sprinkled bits of information about himself into the conversation. He made it clear that he was well-to-do; he went to such-and-such four-star restaurants, he had connections with so-and-so, he weekended on the Island, and so on and so on.

The unwanted attention annoyed Lauren, but it achieved Brian's goal, which was to draw attention to himself. His pretensions to be understated as he advertised himself did not fool Lauren. She sized him up silently. I've seen your type thousands of times before, she said to herself; good-looking, successful, but thinks too much of himself, thinks that every woman wants to be with him. Brian was pushing hard to win Lauren over, but she kept deflecting his advances. She thought him to be vain and tiresome, someone she didn't like. Nevertheless, Lauren remained polite with Brian, but her patience began to wear thin after a while. When she couldn't take it anymore, she executed a common defensive maneuver. She excused herself and went to the ladies' room.

Brian, for all of his shortcomings, was a smart guy. He could see that his usual modus operandi was going nowhere, and that he needed to regroup and fashion another mode of attack. He was a bit of a shark when it came to dating, and he was very good at getting the woman that he wanted. He had many acts which were well rehearsed, "I'm good-looking, rich and successful", "I'm sensitive", "I just need somebody right now", among others. Now that his first act was not successful, it was time to move onto the next act.

When Lauren came back to the party, Brian left her alone and watched her carefully, waiting for a moment to move back in. She walked up to a statuesque blonde who was at the bar, evidently waiting for her drink. Lauren must have been good friends with her; they hugged each other spiritedly as only close friends do, and soon they were talking animatedly and laughing over something that was whispered between them. Brian's mind, as was natural with him, turned a few curves south as he watched them. He wondered if he could get both of them in bed with him. I could show them what a man's really about, he thought, man, they were both so hot!

Lauren and her friend left the bar and went out to the large balcony overlooking the city. "It's beautiful out here," she murmured. The balcony looked out toward the northern night sky. The city park was immediately before her, a large expanse of darkness extending into the distance. It was impossible to make out the shapes of even the nearest trees in the night. The park was outlined by lights shining from the buildings around its perimeter. There were a few lights twinkling in the distance, scattered amidst the quiet landscape. In the night sky, the park looked like a painting in which tiny beacons of light, tiny rays of hope and kindness, were scattered among the dark landscape; and the entire canvas was framed by the soft glow of the city.

Lauren and her friend talked for a while on the balcony, admiring the night sky and the insomniac city below. Her friend suddenly recognized a face in the crowd, and she yelled out his name and waved to him. He made his way to them and exchanged a peck on the cheek with the blonde. They talked for a little while with Lauren, then they came inside for another drink, leaving Lauren alone. Brian, who had followed them out into the balcony, saw his second chance and went up to Lauren.

"Hi again," he said politely. "You know, I think I owe you an apology, I think I was rather rude back there. It's just that I really wanted to talk to you, and I was really nervous and I wasn't myself. I didn't mean to come off as such a jerk."

Lauren was always a softie, and she accepted Brian's apology. Brian began his second act, and a practiced look of contrition appeared on his handsome face as he spoke. He played his role well, they talked mostly about her, he shied away from talking about himself. He played the attentive listener, smiled appropriately, always respecting her distance.

Slowly and surely, Lauren began to look at Brian in a not so deprecating light. Certainly, he was a very good-looking man, and had a great physique. He was self-confident, but now she could see that he was really a nice person once you got over his false bravado. Brian continued to act his part as they talked together, and Lauren's defenses slowly melted away.

Brian asked Lauren if he may take her home as the party winded down. She had too nice a talk with him to refuse outright, and she acquiesced. He hailed a cab and they made their way to her place. They continued to chat in the car amiably.

Brian knew how to play his cards right. When the taxi arrived at her apartment, he got out quickly and opened her door. There was a sweet smile in his face as he helped her out of the car. He asked the cab driver to wait as he walked her to her door. He held her hands gently as he asked if he may call her, and perhaps get together for dinner. By this time Lauren had forgotten how he acted when she first met him, and they exchanged phone numbers. "I'm really looking forward to it," he said beamingly. He raised her hand to his lips and asked her if he may give her a kiss. She smiled. He kissed her hand, pretended to be unwilling to let go, and then said goodnight. He walked back toward the cab, knowing that she was watching him, knowing that she was expecting him to turn back for another longing glance. True to the test, he turned back and admired her lovingly from the curb, smiling dashingly, then he reluctantly entered the cab and they drove off.

He knew that he had made a good impression. I have to be careful with this one, he thought. It may be a few dates before I can get her in the sack, I have to play my cards right. Feeling smug, he had the cab driver take him to an off-hours club that he knew. There, he found a brunette willing to play his game, and they spent the night together.

Contrary to the popular image of models, Lauren did not go out every night, not even on weekends.

Lauren grew up in a suburb outside of Philadelphia, on the "main line". She would tell you that she had a pretty uneventful childhood, with the exception of a broken arm when she was five. Her friends were her neighbors. They were down-to-earth, nice, grounded girls. Lauren was a cute little girl who ran around the park getting dirty, laughing, out of breath, perfectly happy. She loved playing catch with her dad and her younger sister, and she would be the first to admit that she was more interested in running around the field than shopping for pretty clothes.

It was not nature's intention to hold back Lauren's beauty. She became more and more beautiful as she grew into her early teens. Lauren still was not into "girlie things", as she would say. She never wore makeup to school, and her attire was usually a clean T-shirt and a pair of jeans. She wasn't glamorous, but she was naturally pretty. She kept up her grades, played on the volleyball team (she was getting tall), practiced her piano every now and then, and didn't pay any attention to the boys at all.

There were always a million ways of being "discovered." In Lauren's case, there was a friend of a friend of her mom who she remembered meeting once at someone's wedding. Mrs. Corvo was a little surprised when Diane approached her about her daughter. She was certainly proud of Lauren, but she couldn't help being a little surprised that someone regarded her little girl as beautiful enough to be a model, and she was a little apprehensive at the thought of her little girl taking such a step. Despite her misgivings, she wasn't the type of mom who kept opportunities from her daughter. She trusted her daughter too much to hold anything back from her, and she really wanted Lauren to make her own decisions. Mrs. Corvo spoke to her husband about it and he was supportive of the idea. He understood her apprehensions, and left the final say to his wife to decide.

A few days later, Mrs. Corvo spoke to Lauren. It was about mid-afternoon and Lauren had just gotten back from school about half an hour ago. She was busily working on some Algebra, trying to get her homework out of the way so she could meet her friend Andrea for tennis later that evening. Lauren broke her concentration when she heard her mom's knock on the door. Mrs. Corvo came in and was greeted by a "Hi, mom!" and a welcoming smile from her daughter. Lit by the sunlight filtering through the window next to her desk, the daughter was as lovely and beautiful as ever. She walked over to Lauren's desk and Lauren pointed out that she was doing math homework. Mrs. Corvo smiled, sat down next to her and spoke to her about Diane. Lauren was rather nonchalant at the idea. "Sure," she answered, "it sounds like fun."

That was the beginning. She didn't become a princess overnight, but her life slowly went through some big changes. She learned about modeling, makeup, looking pretty, walking like a lady. She still remembered how exciting it was at that first photo session, sitting there while a hundred people busied themselves around her, transforming her from a girl to a model. Even she was a little awed at her appearance when they were finished. Then there was her first fashion show, how she thought she would be so unbelievably nervous, but somehow she remained calm as she strode down the runway, unfazed by the thousands of eyes watching her in the dark. She remembered driving home with her parents afterwards, and looking over her Bio notes in the car because she had a big test the next day.

There was less time for tennis and more time spent traveling to New York. She didn't have to ask her dad for money for movies any more. She was paid an incredible amount of money (so it seemed to her) and her parents set aside a tiny portion of it for her to use at her own discretion. She didn't run out and buy a car, but she was able to treat her friends to pizza and movies on the weekends. Lauren paid for the movie tickets, her friends got the popcorn and soda, and they continued to be nice, down-to-earth girls.

If the boys didn't notice how pretty Lauren was before, they noticed her now as news of her modeling career slowly made its way around the school. Some of her classmates thought her a snob because she wasn't interested in dating anyone, but the boys that she was friends with still knew her to be a nice girl and a loyal friend. It was more fun to hang out with her friends watching their favorite TV shows or to stay at home and play *Trivial Pursuit* with her family.

Lauren was taking some classes at the university near where she lived in the city. At the time, she was at a peak in her modeling career. She was in constant demand and she worked a lot, putting in many hours each week, but she still made some free time to work toward getting a degree. She would be glad that she did this in the future, she said to herself. Her parents were happy that she was taking classes, and it was a good change of pace, most of the time, unless there was a big assignment or a big exam coming up. Sometimes she had to miss a class in order to go to a shoot, but she still spent enough time at school to make it worthwhile.

On some nights, she would just stay in and do a little studying, watch a movie, call her parents. Her friend Andrea was finishing law school at the same university and they would often go out for a late night coffee or snack when Andrea needed to get out from under the books. It was nice to have a close friend from home in the city; there was a degree of intimacy and candor which was special between two best friends.

"So, how are things going with Brian?" asked Andrea, as they settled into a corner of the cafe which they frequented.

"It's good," Lauren paused. "We're going out on Saturday."

"Hmm, why the hesitation?"

"Well, you know, it's the same old thing," said Lauren, pouring milk into her coffee. "He wants to spend the night together, and you know me."

Andrea knew exactly what Lauren meant. Lauren, in her own way, was waiting for someone special. It wasn't that she was a virgin. She had had two lovers in the past. Her first time was an awkward, somewhat painful experience just after high school. Her second lover wasn't much better. It was obvious to her, in retrospect, that sex was foremost, if not the only thing, on their minds, and that they were rather lacking as a companion or a friend. She wanted the next time to be with someone special, perhaps that someone whom everyone was searching for. Then, perhaps, the physical relationship would be special, too. Andrea often kidded her about it, about "her stance against men", as she phrased it. Despite the teasing, Lauren's attitude toward sex was also one of those things that Andrea respected about her friend. It was a romantic notion, but it wasn't for everybody.

"You don't think he's the one?" asked Andrea.

"I don't know. Sometimes he feels right, and sometimes, well …" she trailed off.

"Well what?"

"Sometimes … I just get a strange feeling about him sometimes." answered Lauren.

Andrea had never liked Brian. She didn't know exactly what it was about him, but she never trusted him from the moment that Lauren introduced him to her. There was something in the way that he try to win her over that was too artificial. She didn't like his quiet boasting, which he thought went undetected but was only too obvious. She didn't like the way that Brian looked at other women; she didn't liked the way that she caught Brian looking at her sometimes. It caused her to believe that he could not be trusted, that he would be unfaithful to her good friend.

But, as was so often the case, Andrea kept her suspicions and her thoughts to herself. It's never clear why even the best of friends, who could share the most intimate details of their lives, would withhold such an important opinion to themselves. Perhaps it was better to let her make her own decisions, be it right or wrong. Perhaps there was something that you didn't know about him. Perhaps if they ended up together, it would become an awkward barrier in your future relationship. Perhaps it was too difficult to talk about.

These situations sometimes work out for the best, but more often than not, they lead to unhappy endings.

"Do you want to get together for dinner tomorrow?" asked Andrea.

"I thought you were having a quiet night in with Peter." Peter was Andrea's fiancé; a nice guy, an investment banker, which meant frequent time away.

"He had to go to Denver yesterday. He'll be away until the end of next week."

"I can't," answered Lauren, "I'm having dinner with someone."

"Who?"

"Someone I met just the other day."

Andrea looked at her friend cautiously, trying to read more between the lines. Lauren remained silent, smiling mischievously as she took a sip of her coffee.

"Uh, a little more information, please," asked Andrea.

Lauren told Andrea about her lunch with James. She described their meeting excitedly, recalling the many small, vivid details of the day. Andrea noticed with satisfaction that there was a beam in Lauren's eyes and a lilt in her voice as she spoke. Lauren was happy.

"That was rather romantic, wasn't it?" said Andrea to Lauren.

Lauren contemplated thoughtfully. "I guess it was. It sure was."

On her way home, Andrea thought about James, the man that she had yet to meet. He seemed to be quite a nice guy. Maybe he'll be the one, she thought, maybe he'll be the one.

James called Lauren the next day after their lunch together. He was a little nervous about calling her. After all, it wasn't everyday that he called someone that he dreamt about spending the rest of his life with. His mind worked furiously before he called, trying to think of a nice place where they could have a quiet, romantic first date. Should he go all out and go for one of those famously romantic restaurants? One of those places where people go for a once in a lifetime moment, often to propose to their sweethearts over soft music. Or would she rather have dinner in a small, intimate cafe? They could make it their place, a place that they could treasure forever, and smile thoughtfully to each other every time they dine there, or even when they pass by. What kind of food does she like? Does she like wine, or would she rather have a hot cup of sake? The questions went on and on. Decisions were endless when he wanted everything to be perfect.

Deep in his heart, James knew that, as much as he wanted to have a perfect little dinner planned, it probably didn't matter to Lauren whether they went to the famously romantic restaurant or the little cafe around the corner. To be honest, he knew it didn't matter so much to him either. After all, it was the company that made the dinner special. He himself would be happy to be anywhere, if Lauren were there with him. Realizing this, he decided to just call Lauren, and they could make plans together.

It was late morning. Lauren had just returned from the gym when the phone rang. She picked up the phone and James's voice echoed through the receiver.

"Hi, Lauren?"

"Hey James! How are you?" answered Lauren.

She recognized his voice! The thought instantly sent a shiver of delight down his spine. A smile rose in his face, unseen over the telephone. She was glad to hear from him! How delightful that voice was!

James had the day off. He had slept poorly the night before. He had been daydreaming about Lauren since he left her at lunch. He wondered if she would be interested in him. The sweet memory of their meeting was replayed time and again. It would be so nice to finally find someone to love, someone who loved him. It was premature, to be sure, to jump to such conclusions, but how sweet that would be.

He fell asleep thinking about Lauren that night, and she was the first thing on his mind when he woke up the next morning. He had to collect his thoughts before he could make sure that, yes, he did have lunch with an angel yesterday, and yes, he had to call her later to make dinner plans for Friday. Friday! Not Monday, not Wednesday, not Sunday, but Friday-the day for romance, the day where couples meet and discover each other.

James got up from his bed with a smile on his face. He was happy. It took so little to be happy sometimes. He pulled up his shorts and walked to bathroom, washing his face with warm water. He looked at himself carefully in the mirror as he ran the electric shaver over his face. Not a bad mug, he thought. Happiness and self-esteem seemed to go hand-in-hand.

On his days off, James liked to run in the park. James did it more for the exercise than anything else. He didn't particularly enjoy running. It was rather monotonous, as far as sports go, but it was an easy way to keep the heart and the body in shape.

James liked to run in the morning. It took him little time to wake up and get ready in the morning. He would have a little milk after he washed up, and then put on his running shorts and T-shirt. He usually wore a cap so that he didn't need to take the time to comb his hair before he went out. He would do his run, then come back, have some breakfast, shower, and then either nap a little or go on with his day. It was a good way to start a day off.

He ran on a path that circled a reservoir in the park. The track used to be pretty beaten up in places, but a major renovation a few years ago rejuvenated the jogging path. Now it was in pretty good shape even after a heavy rain or snow. It was not so bad even when the snow melted into ice. The loop around the reservoir was about a mile and a half. It was perfect for a lazy day when he didn't feel like running much; such as when the weather was humid or below freezing, or when he got out to run just because he hadn't exercised for a little while. It was also perfect when he felt like running, extending his mile and a half into three, four and a half, or six miles. The trail offered an unobstructed view of the park as it looped around the reservoir. It was easy to see where you began, how far along you were, and where you were heading on the trail. Since you usually had to end up where you started, you couldn't just quit running when you were tired if you were far away from your starting point, because then you'd have a long walk back.

James sometimes broke the monotony by counting how many people he passed, or how many people passed him. Sometimes he followed someone around the track, keeping with their pace, which was usually faster, slower, or longer than what he had intended. There was a time that he followed a beautiful woman around the track, and then he ran longer than he ever did, a whole nine miles, and probably could have gone on longer than that.

James ran his usual three miles that morning. Thoughts raced in and out of his mind as he ran. How much longer to go? How far is that old man running? Wow, that woman is running pretty fast. When is my next day at work? I have to call Lauren later. Thoughts of Lauren kept interjecting into his usual random train of thought as he ran.

James' favorite part about running was finishing. It felt all right when he was running, but it felt great when he was done. The slight ache in his body was gratifying. It felt good to wipe the sweat off his face with his T-shirt. It felt good to have completed something. It made him stronger, and he was satisfied with himself as he walked home from the park.

Lauren and James talked about seemingly random subjects, but the course of the conversation was seamless. She was at the gym in the morning. She did a little bit of everything at the gym. This morning was yoga. Yoga looked easy, he said, but it's probably harder than it seems. Skiing is like that to me, she said, the good skiers make it look so effortless. She skis blues and greens. He's a decent skier. I would love to go skiing together some time. You wouldn't be taking me down any cliffs, would you? He wouldn't do that! He was a good ski buddy, he protested. What do you do in the summer when you're not skiing? I like to hike, and I run a little to keep in shape. I ran in the park this morning. The reservoir? I like to run around the reservoir too. Have you been to the boat house? I've never been there either. I think you can rent rowboats there. It looks like fun. He gets seasick on boats, but he's fine on canoes and kayaks. Hey, maybe we can have dinner at the boat basin. Where is that? What's it like? It sounds like fun. I'll meet you there Friday.

As simple as that, the plans were made.

James got there a little early, as usual. He wore a blue knit polo and a pair of olive khakis. The weather was sunny and clear during the day, but the evening brought the mild chill of early fall. He took a light fleece pullover with him in case if it got too chilly.

It was often a little uncomfortable waiting for your date, particularly a first date. James twittered around the fountain near the outdoor cafe. He didn't want to get a drink at the bar. He didn't want to drink too much when he was with Lauren. Sometimes he said or did stupid things when he had a little too much to drink.

James didn't have to wait too long, Lauren showed up a little early as well. She had never been to the boat basin before, and she gave herself a little extra time in case she got lost. She didn't want to have James waiting for too long. He was so happy to see her, his heart raced. She looked wonderful. Lauren wore a light green dress that clinged beautifully to her body, but she could have worn anything as far as James was concerned. It wasn't what she was wearing that was so wonderful to him, it was what was inside the dress that mattered; it was her. She smiled brightly and waved to James as she walked down the stairs to the cafe. The slight anxiety that James felt while he was waiting disappeared instantly.

"This place looks wonderful. It's my first time here."

The boat basin was an outdoor bar and cafe in a narrow strip of parkland which ran along the bank of the river. The restaurant was set in a sunken garden which concealed it completely from view from the populace of the city. Unless one was looking for it, it was easy to overlook the secluded cafe amid the oaks and the maples. It was a pleasant surprise for those who were fortunate enough to have stumbled upon it. It was like a tiny treasure, hidden away, waiting to be discovered.

Inside the small park, there was a small, difficult to see sign that pointed to the staircases which led down to the boat basin. The staircases flanked in opposite directions, slowly winding their way around a granite plaza before descending to the boat basin. A small, ornately decorated fountain sat silently in the middle of the plaza. The small plaza was reminiscent of a familiar place where people gathered. The plaza opened up to the west, affording a panoramic view of the river and the small hills on the opposite bank. The cafe was recessed in this area, so that the guests were able to appreciate the waters as they sat at their tables.

James and Lauren took a short stroll through the grounds. They walked around the quiet fountain, examining the sculptures more with mirth than seriousness. They liked the way the staircases encircled the plaza. James led Lauren through the bar and they descended to the edge of the water, watching the current flow gently down the river. They leaned on the railing and looked into the distance upstream, where the foliage was donning its fall colors in earnest. They took in the view silently, each with their thoughts, enjoying the lovely vista. It was a moment when words were not needed. Their thoughts were one, though independent. Lauren and James turned and smiled at each other, and walked back toward the cafe.

The boat basin was not too crowded for a Friday night. It might have been a bit cold, but Lauren and James didn't notice it at all. They were seated quickly.

James suggested sharing a bottle of wine. They have some nice Chardonnays, Lauren said.

"Your favorite?" asked James, remembering she had Chardonnay at lunch.

"How did you know?"

"Just a hunch," he answered.

The waitress returned with their wine.

"Here's to new friends," James toasted.

Lauren raised her glass. Their glasses clinked melodically. She looked into his eyes and smiled inwardly; that was a wonderful toast, a wonderful sentiment. It wasn't too difficult to see that they could become good friends, she thought.

The sun was setting across the river as they sat with their drinks. Silently, they watched the light bounce off speckles of yellow and red scattered among the trees. Slowly, the sun disappeared bit by bit behind the hills. The bright orange sphere became three-quarters, then a half, then a crescent. As the sun waned in the evening, the sky lit up with rays of red and orange as the sunlight scattered through the thin clouds far off on the horizon. The sky was brilliant with an intense red hue for a few minutes before it burnt itself out, and twilight began to settle in.

"Beautiful," James said. It was Lauren's thoughts exactly.

The evening passed quickly. They talked and talked and talked. Sometimes it was surprising how a simple conversation could be so enjoyable. It didn't seem like they had talked for hours, but they did. They shared all the little details of their lives with each other; her family was in Pennsylvania, she loved playing tennis, she was going to school part time. Lauren even revealed that she worked as a model. "Now I have to kill you," she told him. James laughed.

The night crept in softly. A slight breeze off the water brought goosebumps to the skin. It was getting cold. James was oblivious to the cold, just as he was oblivious to everything but Lauren. She shivered when the wind picked up a bit and James offered her his fleece. As much as he hated to leave, he saw that Lauren was getting too cold to be comfortable, even with his jacket. This time, James insisted on picking up the tab and Lauren conceded him this small pleasure. They walked back through the darkened park together. Lauren took her leave as they reached the avenue. "I had a great time," she told him. He looked into her eyes and his heart throbbed, yearning to touch her, yearning to hold her against him. "I'll grab a cab home," she smiled. He hailed a taxi for her and held the door open for her. She gave him a hug and a soft kiss on the cheek before getting into the cab. "Goodnight," she waved, and the taxi sped away with her.

Lauren was happy. James was nice. They really hit it off. There was one thing which bothered her as the cab made its way home. Should she have told James about Brian? Was she leading him on? After all, she wasn't engaged or married or anything like that. She didn't lie to him. James never asked her if she were seeing anyone. Yet, somehow she felt that she was being dishonest with James, and it gnawed at her.

James invited Lauren over for dinner the following week. James liked cooking. He liked cooking for his dates, he liked showing off his domestic skills. He believed that women liked guys who could cook, guys who could help around the house. He thought it would help him earn some brownie points in his favor.

The dishes that he made were always pretty simple, but they were always quite wonderful. The key to a good dish was the quality of the ingredients; that was his cooking mantra. Fresh meat, fresh veges, lightly seasoned, prepare it to bring out the natural flavor of the food. Like all good cooks, he had a list of markets that he liked for meats, produce, fish, fruits. He had a few dishes that he knew was well-liked by everyone: stuffed mushrooms, grilled marinated flank steak, fish with lemon-dill, various Chinese stir-fries, and the unfortunately named "shells of death", which was particularly popular.

James was always on the lookout for new recipes, but he still liked to keep things simple. He didn't like recipes with too many ingredients, or recipes with hard-to-find ingredients. He experimented frequently in the kitchen, not always with positive results. He liked to try new recipes on himself a few times before he made them for his guests. He often got it right on the first try, but sometimes his first attempt was somewhat disappointing.

Lauren was coming over on Tuesday. He was going to make her dinner and she would bring a movie. She asked him what kind of movies he liked, but before he answered, she guessed that he probably liked comedies, maybe with a little bit of romance. She was right. He liked sappy movies, the sappier the better, he said.

"What's your favorite movie?" she asked.

"*When Harry Met Sally*," he answered. "You know, I lived through part of that movie."

"What do you mean?"

"Well, once I went on a blind date with this girl, and she wanted to try this deli. We were having pastrami sandwiches when she started moaning, just like this." James then proceeded to act out the famous deli scene from the movie, doing his best impersonation of Sally over the telephone. "I was so embarrassed that I didn't know what to do."

"Oh, shut up, this did not happen."

"It's hard to believe, but it's true."

Lauren laughed. "Hmm, I guess then we'd better not go to any delis together."

"I guess not."

James decided to make fish with lemon-dill, couscous, and carrots and asparagus. He had made the fish many times before, so he knew that it would come out well. The fish market had some good looking perch that day, so he was set with the main course. The couscous was easy to make. It was basically straight out of a box, though he added a little curry to it to give it an exotic flavor. The carrots and asparagus were easy to do, as long as you could find good asparagus. He used baby carrots and julienned them, then trimmed the asparagus. He sautéed them with some olive oil, lemon juice, a little sage, a smidgen of butter, and some salt.

James rarely made dessert, perhaps because there were only a few things that he knew how to make. He usually had some ice cream and fruit handy in case someone wanted sweets. He already had some vanilla ice cream in the freezer, so he bought some fresh blueberries from the supermarket. It was a favorite combination of his.

James was just putting the fish onto the broiler when Lauren arrived. She wore a light gray T-shirt with a small embroidered *Glacier Park* logo and a pair of jeans. She gave James a big hug and a friendly kiss on his cheek, bringing a flush of color to his face. She saw him blushing and smiled to herself.

"I brought back your fleece," she said. "Thanks for letting me use it the other night."

"No problem." James hung the fleece in a closet and returned to the living room, where Lauren was looking over his books.

Lauren was excited about the dinner invitation. Her dates usually chose to take her out to restaurants, and this was a rather nice change of pace. Reflecting back, she couldn't remember the last time one of her dates cooked for her, and certainly never as the main event on a date.

It was easy for her to imagine James in the kitchen. He seemed to have the temperament for a chef, not that Lauren knew what that was, but she knew that he was patient, caring, and kind; elements that she thought would be useful to a chef. There was a bit of an artistic side in him as well, willing to try new things, an ability to create and concoct novel tastes. She could not imagine Brian cooking in the kitchen.

It was also an opportunity to see James' apartment. She always learned a lot about people from where they lived, no matter how artificially tidy the home may be. Books, music, photos, pictures on the wall; these said a lot about the people who lived there. James' bookshelf was a menagerie of mostly classics mixed with a few contemporary novels. Two of her favorite books sat together on the top shelf, *To Kill a Mockingbird* and *Love Story*. His music collection was an eclectic blend of artists known and unknown from every genre: jazz, contemporary, soul, rap, classical, hard rock, country. She thought it was funny to see Carole King sitting next to Pink Floyd.

"Dinner is almost ready, would you like some wine?"

"Sure, that sounds great." James opened a bottle of Sauvignon Blanc that was chilling in the fridge and filled two jade-tinted wine glasses.

"This is good, what is it?"

"It's a Sauvignon Blanc. I thought we could try something different. What do you think?"

"I like it, it's pretty good."

James checked on the fish. It was ready. He took it out of the broiler and drizzled the light lemon-dill sauce over the fish. Then he plated the fish with the couscous and the veges, and they sat down to the small dining table together.

"Mmm, everything smells so good. What kind of fish is that?"

Lauren was definitely impressed. Everything was delicious, and she delighted James with her compliments. They chatted amicably over dinner, talking about their day, the boat basin, James' apartment.

Lauren helped James clear the dishes. "That was really good, so what else can you make me for dinner?" Lauren asked, laughing at her own jest.

Nothing would please James more than to cook for Lauren again and again.

"So what movie did you bring?" asked James.

"*Cousins.*"

"What's it about?."

"I think you'd like it. Love, romance, happiness, that sort of thing; at least that's what the box says. How can you go wrong with that?"

They nestled onto the couch and started the movie, sitting close to each other. The movie *was* about love, romance, happiness, that sort of thing. It was sad at times, but ultimately there was a happy ending. Lauren and James looked mistily toward each other after the happy ending.

"That *was* pretty good."

They turned off the movie and chatted over some wine. Lauren asked him about the pictures hanging in his living room. They were beautiful landscapes; photographs of valleys, lakes, and mountains. James liked hiking outdoors, and he was slowly working his way to see all of the National Parks. The pictures were enlargements of shots that he had taken during his travels. Lauren recognized a photograph of a series of glaciated valleys from Glacier Park. She went there with her sister a couple of years ago, and the T-shirt that she wore was a treasured souvenir from the trip. James had visited there the year before, and they talked about where they stayed, where they hiked, all the animals they saw, and on and on.

They talked for a long time, finding more and more in common with each other. Tennis, hiking, skiing, Jane Austen, sushi. Lauren remembered that James had gone to college in Philadelphia. They talked about South Street, Reading Terminal, Fairmount Park. It was past one in the morning before they realized how late it had gotten.

"I have to go. I have a class in the morning." said Lauren, checking her watch. She gathered her things and James walked her to the door.

She caressed him on the shoulder and kissed him on the cheek again.

"Thanks for dinner, that was great."

"Thanks for the movie."

It was one of the most enjoyable evenings that Lauren had in a long while. The night was unfettered by sexual tension or awkward moments. She never felt that she needed to be on her guard. She was completely relaxed and at ease with James. It was a wonderful evening from which an intimate friendship would blossom, a friendship which would change their lives.

Lauren and James continued to see each other over the next few weeks, and their friendship grew quickly. They bonded over things important and trivial, and they always had a great time when they went out together. Some weeks later, Lauren asked James to go on a biking trip with her. On Sundays in the fall, one of the parkways near the city was closed down to traffic for bicyclists. Lauren had always wanted to try it out, but she never found someone enthusiastic to accompany her. She asked James if he were interested, and he loved the idea. James said it sounded like fun; the weather was supposed to be nice, and it was another chance to spend more time with Lauren.

The parkway followed the course of a small brook which wound its way through the lush countryside. Breathing in the fresh air, listening to the quiet sounds of the woodlands, it was hard to keep in mind that the busy cityscape laid only a few minutes away. It was not so difficult to find peace and tranquility away from the frenzy of everyday life after all. It was not so far away.

The foliage was now in bloom in earnest. Reds, oranges, yellows covered the trees all along the parkway, painting a rather scenic backdrop for the bicyclists. They passed other cyclists as they leisurely pedaled along the road, meeting families of moms, dads, smiling and waving to their children, some with ribbons and flags on their bicycles, some still in their training wheels. There were a few lone riders, some racing down the parkway in pursuit of who knows what, some were stopped along the parkway, sitting in the sun, watching the sparse traffic pass by. There were couples riding side by side, leisurely making their way with no destination in mind, much like themselves, content with the journey, content with being together.

They came to a creek which crossed the parkway. They stopped and left the road, walking their bikes along the bank of the creek. The sun sparkled in the trickling water, splashing shadows across the stream. They found a smooth rock near the creek and sat down for a rest. James picked up a pebble and skipped it across the creek, skimming the surface three times before sinking into the water. Lauren picked up a stone and tossed it into the water, but it sunk when it hit the surface of the creek. Lauren picked up another rock and tried it again, with the same "plunk" for a result. James found her a better shaped stone, and showed her how to throw it side-arm along the surface of the water. Lauren's third attempt was unsuccessful as well, but on the next try, the pebble skipped across the water twice, and she let out an ecstatic cry at her achievement. She met with much better success after that, getting the stones to skip twice, then three times, then four, delighting each time that she broke her own record. James and Lauren spent the next half hour skipping stones together, and they laughed joyfully each time both stones skipped four or five times together. Who knew that skipping rocks could be so much fun?

They got up and walked further along the creek. It became quieter. Soon Lauren and James were alone, their fellow bicyclists left behind. They came across a small island in the creek. There were a few rocks in the riverbed that made a precarious bridge to the islet. They made their way together toward the first rock. Lauren looked at James, and James looked at Lauren. James stretched out a foot on the first rock and put a little pressure on it, testing its stability, then he stepped onto it easily. He took a big stride and made his way to the second rock, and Lauren followed suit. Slowly they made their way across the stream. James was the first to land on the small island. There was a little bit of a jump from the last rock to the island. He held out his hand to Lauren. Lauren tightened her legs and launched herself off the last rock, over-jumping the shore and falling into James with a thud. James caught her in his arms as she crashed into him, the two of them teetering backwards for a step or two. She was so warm and so lovely as he held her against him. He wanted to kiss her right there, the moment was perfect. They gazed deeply into each other's eyes, their faces so close together that their lips were almost touching. It would take no effort at all to close that small distance. James moved to kiss her. Lauren waited for him, not drawing back, but for some reason he hesitated. Suddenly they were unsure, suddenly the moment was faltering, suddenly they felt embarrassed. They broke their embrace and separated.

They walked around the island together, tracing their footsteps along the pebbly shore. Neither of them said much. They found a cozy grassy space shaded under some cedars and had a picnic there. Lauren unrolled a small blanket and they sat down on the soft ground. They ate their sandwiches listening to the gentle babble of the creek, interrupted now and then by a songbird invisible to their eyes. Lauren laid out on the blanket after she finished her lunch, and James laid down next to her. They stared up at the sky together. The leaves fluttered when a soft wind blew. A hawk soared high overhead, disappearing from one treetop to another. Clouds drifted by, or rather, they strolled through the sky, lighting the imaginations of the two people laying far beneath them. One was a flower, one was a sweetbun, one was a teacup, as James and Lauren interpreted the shapes for each other. Soon, they were chatting as amicably and as freely as ever. The awkwardness that had insinuated itself between the two friends had dissipated quickly.

On their way back, Lauren wanted to cross the creek by herself. She jumped ahead of James as they approached the rocks that they crossed over. She declined his offer to go first and help her across. James was left to watch her attempt the crossing. She missed the long leap to the first rock and landed in the water, getting both of her feet wet. A little flustered, she took a long stride toward the next rock, her wet sneaker slipped off the edge of the rock and she fell into the creek. She sat in the cold water, angry at herself for falling. James walked into the creek beside Lauren and helped her up. She muttered a soft expletive as she brushed the debris from her backside.

"You didn't need to do that," she said, with a tinge of resentment in her voice, "I could have gotten up. You didn't need to get yourself all wet for no reason."

James was at a loss for a reply, so he kept silent.

Lauren climbed back onto the rocks, and hurriedly scampered across to the other side of the creek. James followed her. He didn't know whether he should apologize for trying to help her. It seemed to be a strange thing to apologize for. He mulled it over and didn't say anything. She was rather quiet as they made their way back on their bikes. She didn't look at him at all as he rode beside her. He was wondering if she was mad at him.

As heavy as the silence was, it was lifted.

Lauren turned to James when they were about half way back along the parkway.

"That was a lot of fun," she said, "I'm glad you came with me."

James turned to Lauren when she spoke. She was smiling. A sincere, warm, bright smile.

"I'm glad I came," he answered.

They didn't speak much the rest of the way back, but now the silence was no longer threatening, the silence was friendly.

When they finished their bike ride, James asked Lauren to dinner again, as they were securing their bikes to the car for the drive home.

"How about dinner Friday?"

"I can't," answered Lauren.

A silence hung gloomily in Lauren's mind. She had to tell James about Brian; she had plans with him that weekend. There was no way around the inevitable subject. It was time, but she was afraid of hurting him.

"I'm going away to the Adirondacks with my boyfriend this weekend." Lauren could sense the dejection on his face as the words trembled from her lips.

Boyfriend! What a horrible word that was to James. All of his fondest hopes were dashed by that one word.

"Oh well. Maybe we can get together another time," James answered, mustering all his strength to suppress his sense of disappointment.

What had been a beautiful afternoon crashed down dismally around James. She has a boyfriend. Again, he must settle for second best. She was never interested in him. Oh, why had he been dreaming? Why was he kidding himself all that time?

There was a tremendous downturn in his spirits. James spoke very little on the way back home, mostly to keep up the conversation out of politeness. Lauren felt as if she had broken his heart, and in fact, she had.

James didn't call Lauren the week after she went to the Adirondacks. She didn't call him either. Another week passed by without a word between them. As much as James tried to put Lauren out of his mind, she would constantly rise to the surface. It was as if the harder he tried to forget her, to forget what happened, the more intense the memories of her became.

There was a message from Lauren on his answering machine the following week.

"Hey James, it's me, Lauren. Just calling to say hi. I've been pretty busy, but I wanted to see how you were doing. I had a couple of shoots last week and a big test in school. Anyway, I'm going out with a couple of friends to celebrate at this bar tonight, and it'd be great if you could come. Or maybe we can do something this weekend if it's good for you. Call me back, okay?"

He was surprised to hear that she still wanted to see him. He was not surprised to feel that he wanted to see her too, but he was surprised at how intensely he wanted to see her again.

James called Lauren right back. They were as carefree as before when they spoke to each other, as if nothing had happened to upset their friendship. She had a big midterm that week and she had been studying really hard in between a couple of magazine shoots. She was exhausted but now she was glad it was all over. How was his week? Did he do anything special? James couldn't tell her that he was down and mopey all week. He was working until ten at night that day, but he could meet them afterwards if they were still out. Lauren told him they were meeting at nine, so they'd definitely still be there.

It was a tiring day at work for James. He barely had time to go to the bathroom or eat for twelve hours. He was glad to be getting out of the ER when the time came. He thought about just going home and sleeping, but the thought of Lauren in his mind steered him toward her.

It was almost midnight when he met Lauren at the bar. Lauren yelled out James' name when she saw him. She ran up to him, hugged him too tightly, and did not let go. She rested her head on his shoulders, her long silky hair brushing against his cheek. She hung onto him as if her life depended on it. James was a little embarrassed by this overly warm greeting that drew the attention of all the people in the bar. Everyone was all watching them. It was a little disconcerting, but he was happy to see her, to see that she was happy to see him, and he was happy to be holding Lauren safe in his arms, letting her rest securely in his embrace.

Lauren took James by the hand and led him over to her classmates. She introduced him as her good friend, a title which James was proud to have. Lauren bought a round of *Stoli* for everyone and insisted that James take two shots to "catch up". Lauren and her friends had been drinking quite a bit before he arrived, and she wanted him to join them in their intoxication.

James was the only one who stayed sober at the party. He declined to have more alcohol after his two shots, settling for ginger ale instead. Lauren kept plying him with liquor, but he told her that he was too tired to drink, and would fall asleep in the bar.

The party had quieted down by two in the morning as Lauren's friends began to take their leave. It was obvious to everyone including Lauren herself that she was in no shape to go home alone, so she asked James to take her home. She leaned on James as they made their way out of the bar. He flagged down a cab and kept her from falling as she stumbled into the back seat. She drifted in and out of consciousness as she fell asleep in James' arms during the fifteen minute ride.

James helped Lauren get out of the cab when they got to her place. Lauren took a long time to find her keys, then she had a lot of trouble with the front door. James helped her inside and escorted her into the elevator. He took the keys from her and opened her apartment door for her.

Once in the apartment, Lauren spun herself around and wrapped her arms around James' neck, letting the full weight of her body lean against him.

"You know what? You are a great guy," she said in a drunken voice.

James didn't take her words too seriously, seeing her the way she was. He half-carried her to her bedroom, Lauren still clinging to him, her arms hugging him tightly.

They sat down on the edge of the bed and James untangled himself from Lauren. She giggled as James took off her shoes, then he helped her out of her jacket.

Lauren turned and faced James. "I'm so lucky to have you," she murmured, and unexpectedly, she pulled him close and kissed him on his lips.

James had wished for this kiss ever since they met. It was soft, gentle, warm, and sweet. Lauren looked at James longingly, then she leaned forward and kissed him again, this time forcefully, pushing him down on the bed as she pressed her warm body against him. His flesh was gentle and yielding beneath her, yet he was passionate and full of strength.

For a moment James was lost in heaven, but he didn't lose his head. He knew where he was. He knew better. He rolled himself from under her and sat up on the edge of the bed.

Lauren held his hand tightly and looked up at him. She didn't need to say anything, they both understood that she wanted him to spend the night.

"I think you need some sleep," he said with a sad smile.

James got up from the bed, and Lauren let go of his hand unwillingly. He took a clean T-shirt and cotton pajama pants from her dresser and helped her change out of her clothes. Then James went to the kitchen and got Lauren some water. He made her drink a couple of glasses of water before he put her under the covers. She smiled sweetly at him before quickly drifting off to sleep. James left her in her bedroom when he felt assured that she was going to be safe for the night. He made himself comfortable on her couch where he slept for a few hours. He woke up the next morning, early, and checked on her. She was fine. She was sleeping; she looked so peaceful, so beautiful. James let himself out of the apartment quietly and went to work.

He walked home, feeling very much alone. He could have spent the night with her. It would have been a dream come true. It was something that he wanted badly; it was something that he needed badly. He may never have that chance again. He knew, though, that it was not the right time. He would have never felt right for taking advantage of her like that. No, it was better to suffer alone.

Lauren woke up late the next day. She looked around the bedroom, there was daylight creeping around the edges of the window curtains. She was curled up under her comforter, and somehow she had changed into her pajamas. She was a little achy, but her hangover wasn't too bad. James made her drink a few glasses of water last night, she remembered. James was here last night. She wanted to spend the night with him, she remembered, but he wasn't beside her.

Unbeknownst to James, a lot had happened in the past week with Lauren.

She had a big fight with Brian on the Adirondacks trip. They had stayed in a small bed and breakfast near Saranac Lake. Brian thought that he was finally going to have sex with Lauren that weekend, and he was upset when she made him stay on his side of the bed the first night. They spent the next day hiking, but Brian was sulky. He kept running up the trail ahead of Lauren, leaving her to make her way by herself. He resisted bitterly when she wanted to take a drive to a nearby waterfall. "Why would you want to drive for an hour to see a stupid waterfall?" he demanded. Lauren was becoming exasperated with Brian and her resentment invariably built up inside her. When he tried to have his way with her again that night, she rebuked his advances angrily. A big fight followed. Angry words were exchanged, angry words that had been festering for some time. Brian stormed out of the room and disappeared for the night. Lauren stayed up for a long while before crying herself to sleep. Brian returned in the morning and apologized to her tenderly, but his words were insincere to her. She felt betrayed by his attitude and his actions. His true self had shown itself once too often for her to believe him.

Lauren called Andrea when she came back. She told her what happened over the weekend, and she wept over the phone. Andrea consoled her as best as she could. She would not be sorry to see Brian out of the picture, but she didn't like to see Lauren being so unhappy. She always thought that her friend deserved better. She asked Lauren to have dinner with her. Peter was back and he would love to see her.

It was a mistake to have dinner with Andrea and Peter. Lauren was glad to see Peter; they had always gotten along well, but the dinner only furthered her depression. Despite the best intentions of her friends, it was impossible not to feel a little sad having dinner with them. Seeing them so happy together, and feeling so alone herself after the fight with Brian, she envied her friends more than ever. Andrea and Peter tried their best to entertain her, to get her troubles off her mind, but their efforts were in vain. Lauren put on a brave facade for her friends, but deep inside her, she was sad and unhappy.

She was not her effervescent self at the photo shoots, and her friends noticed it. Only Eric, a photographer, came forward to ask if she was all right. She smiled weakly and told him that she was going through the doldrums, but that she would be fine. It was hard to smile, to be happy, to be glamorous, to be seductive when she was hurting inside. She made it through the shoots drearily, day after day. At night, she buried herself in her books, preparing for the exam that was coming up all too quickly. It was arduous to concentrate on her work, but in a way, she was glad that she had something to take up her time and to divert attention from her misery.

The test came and went. Lauren did pretty well, especially given the circumstances. Her classmates were going out to celebrate. She thought of James. She missed him amid the chaos. She wanted to see him again.

Sure, the alcohol had loosened her inhibitions, but she really did want James to spend the night with her. He was quiet and kind, just the opposite of Brian. She believed him and trusted him, even though she had not known him as long. He would be tender, he would be loving, and he would always be there no matter what.

Lauren slowly aroused herself out of bed. She went into the kitchen and poured herself a glass of orange juice. James wasn't here. She drank it quickly, feeling the cold juice wash down into her body. She sat on the kitchen stool and thought about last night. How did she feel? Was she incredulous that he turned her down? Was she upset? Was she happy? Why did he leave her? What did he think of her? What did he think of her now? Should I call him? Should I apologize? There was nothing to apologize for, was there?

Her phone rang. It was James.

"How are you feeling? Are you okay?" he asked.

"Yes, thanks for helping me home. I just woke up."

"Hey, I'm jealous, I've been at work all morning."

"Listen, I'm sorry …"

"Don't. I was really glad to see you last night. I really missed you."

"Me too, I missed you too," answered Lauren.

"I have to go. I just wanted to check that you were okay, call me tonight?"

"Okay. I'll talk to you later."

James was not as disconsolate later that morning. She kissed him. Maybe she did like him. Maybe there was hope for him yet. He was even more optimistic after speaking to her. He was glad that she was feeling better. He was glad that she missed him. He was glad that she wanted to see him again. James wanted to continue their friendship, no matter which direction the relationship was to take. He was hopeful that their friendship would develop into something much more endearing, but he convinced himself that he would be just as happy being her good friend.

Meanwhile, things were all very up in the air with Brian. He sent her flowers, long-stemmed red roses, the next week, along with a card saying that he was sorry. Lauren was still angry with him and she left his calls unanswered. He sent her more flowers and left her more apologies, begging her to have a face-to-face with him. Lauren was never one to sustain an icy attitude toward someone for long, it was not her personality to be spiteful and unforgiving. Eventually she agreed to have dinner with him, to talk things over. Brian put on his best face to win her back, asking her to forgive him, asking her to give him another chance after all the time that they've had together. She told him that she needed some time to think about it. He made her promise to think things over and reconsider.

In the meantime, Lauren and James were spending more and more time together. The kiss that they shared had seemingly fanned the flames of their relationship to new heights. It wasn't that they became romantically involved, but they became much closer as friends. A day rarely passed by when they did not speak to each other. They saw each other almost every day. They were trying new things together and sharing their special places; museums, picnics, playing catch in the park, movies, favorite restaurants. They did everything together. He met her for dinner after her evening classes. She came over to watch *Gilmore Girls* on Tuesdays. He made dinner for her one day, she made him dinner the next. He came over and read while she studied; they took coffee breaks together. They were inseparable during those few weeks.

They became more intimate, sharing the more important, deeper aspects of their personal lives with each other. Lauren was no longer hesitant over talking to James about Brian. She spoke candidly, about her hopes, her disappointments with Brian. Brian wanted to get back together, but she didn't know if things were ever going to be same. She didn't know what she wanted, she wasn't sure how she felt, she didn't know where they were going, she didn't know if she could trust him, she didn't know if she loved him.

James listened to her patiently. Inwardly, he couldn't help himself from feeling a little pleased at the news of her breakup with Brian, but like Andrea, he was more sorry to see Lauren upset and unhappy. He wanted to tell her to forget about Brian, that he was no good for her, that she deserved someone better, that she should be with someone else. He was ambivalent about expressing his own feelings. He thought that he was too involved in the matter and may give her conflicted advice, because he wanted to take the place as her significant other. He knew that Lauren was not ready to take that next step with him, so he was content to be her friend, listening to her patiently, supporting her decisions faithfully, whatever they may be.

James' best friend Sam lived in Connecticut. They were next-door neighbors freshman year and they developed an easy friendship quickly. They became roommates after freshman year and remained so through graduation. They were both in the engineering school, though different majors. Since they were on similar tracks, they had several classes together. It was fun having friends in the same class, even if it was boring old Chemistry. James would bang on Sam's door when he was late getting up, which was most mornings. They would squeeze into the dormitory elevator, and take the short walk down to the Chemistry building. After lecture, they would meet their other dormmates; Steve, Stacie, Mary Ellen, Lori, Jon, Joy, at the muffin nook and do crosswords together. It was a wonderful routine, day in, day out.

It was inevitable, as close friends, that there were strong influences between them. When he started college, James' major was in Computer Science Engineering. He was really quite good "playing with computers", and it seemed an interesting career. Sam, on the other hand, had wanted to be a doctor. He was a Bioengineering major, but he was really "pre-med", working himself toward medical school. Ever so slowly, James became interested with the idea of becoming a doctor himself. It took little convincing by Sam to push James into that direction. "Monkey see, monkey do," he chimed, whenever he was asked how he became interested in medicine. So, after four years of college, they both went to medical school, James to New York, and Sam to Boston.

Sam was one of the smartest people that James knew. Their small circle of friends often made fun of Sam's ability to sleep through class and still get an A. There was one time when he was snoring so loudly in Organic Chemistry that even the professor heard him. Dr. Mallory stopped in mid-sentence and looked suspiciously toward the back of the huge lecture hall. James and Stacie had to wake him up so that the professor could go on with her lecture. "Was I snoring that loudly?" he asked after class. His friends just laughed.

Time and distance had separated the two friends. Sam had been married for a few years. They still talked on the phone and saw each other occasionally, but it wasn't the same as back when they were both single and unattached. Still, friendships such as theirs have an everlasting warmth that never fades, always ready to be rekindled quickly with a few words.

It was the last weekend in October. Sam was having a barbecue, a last outdoor party before the weather got too cold. James looked forward to seeing his friend and his wife again; it had been a while since he had visited them.

The weather turned out fair that day. James drove up early in the day to play tennis with Sam in the afternoon. Just like back in college, Sam beat James rather easily. It bothered James that he still lost to Sam, even though he was in much better shape than when he was back in college, and Sam had not played tennis for some time. To be fair, Sam had been playing tennis since he was young, and still maintained a solid form from lessons he had way back when. James was a respectable player, but Sam was simply better.

The two friends played tennis for a couple of hours. It was a good bit of exercise, just enough to make them feel like they did something, not enough to make them exhausted. They gathered the fuzzy green balls and made their way back to the house. Sam grabbed a diet cola out of the fridge and handed James a regular cola. "Someday I'm going to convert you," Sam said. He had been trying to get James to convert to diet cola without success ever since freshman year, not that he put much effort into it, neither did James put much effort into resisting. They plopped down on the couch and Sam turned on the TV. He flipped through a few channels before putting down the remote.

An old movie was playing.

"Remember when we saw this movie?" he asked James.

"Sure, it was one of our finals movies."

Back in college, James and Sam always went to see a movie during finals week. Neither of them remembered how the tradition started, or who even came up with the idea. It just happened one semester and they kept the tradition going for no particular reason at all.

They settled into their seats comfortably and watched the movie, making random comments about the movie or whatever happened to come into their heads.

The end of the movie was interrupted by the sound of jangling keys. Kelly was home. The front door opened and closed with a soft bang. Sam and James got up from the sofa; they caught a glimpse of her running into the kitchen with two large bags of groceries. Sam took the bags from his wife while she said her hellos to James. His drive up wasn't too bad. Work was going ok. We played tennis. Your husband beat me again. We were watching a movie.

Sam and Kelly sorted the groceries and started on prepping dinner. Kelly took the shell steaks they were to grill later and started to make a marinade. Sam got started on the potatoes and veges. It was pretty neat to James to see how the couple divided up the work almost wordlessly. They made a good team, he told them. He asked if there was anything he could do to help. Kelly told him to sit there and look pretty.

Sam and Kelly had a few other people over besides James. They were all Connecticut people. There were Sam and Kelly's brothers, Kelly's two best friends, and a couple they knew from Boston. They were all people that James had met before through Sam and Kelly, and the group almost made up most of Sam and Kelly's wedding party. James didn't see them much except at Sam's, but he knew them all and blended pretty well into the group.

The dinner went off splendidly. Afterward, they lingered outdoors with some drinks on the refurnished balcony. Sam and Kelly's place stood along the sandy coast and offered a pretty view of the sea. The waves made a soothing melody in the background as they splashed up on the shore. The small gathering broke up as it got dark, the guests said their goodbyes one by one.

Sam wanted to give James a copy of a CD before he left. "I think it's in the bedroom," he said. One of Kelly's fashion magazines was laying on the desk. James picked up the magazine.

"Hey, I know her," he said, pointing to the familiar face on the magazine cover.

Sam turned his attention from the CD to see who James was talking about.

"Her?" he asked, indicating the woman on the cover.

"Yeah, we went out a couple of times," answered James.

"For real?"

"For real."

"Are you BS-ing me?" asked Sam.

"No kidding."

"You're going out with her, the woman on the cover?"

"Yes, her name is Lauren."

"I can't believe that you didn't say anything about this all day. Hey Kelly, can you come in the bedroom for a second?" Sam called to his wife.

"What's going on? Did you need something?" asked Kelly.

"James is going out with her," Sam said, showing her the magazine.

"Hey, you're going out with someone and you didn't tell me?" she asked with mock indignation. Whenever James visited, Kelly's first few words to James were usually "Hi, great to see you," followed by "So are you dating anyone?" James' usual answer was "nothing to report", accompanied by a barely audible dejected sigh. She had forgotten her friendly interrogation that day because she was busy with the groceries, but she was happily surprised by James' news.

Kelly looked at the magazine. "Are you serious?!? She's pretty famous; she does a lot of modeling." Kelly picked up a couple of magazines from her desk and leafed through the pages, looking for pictures of Lauren. Lauren's face was everywhere, ads for designer clothing, hair products, makeup, everything. "You're dating her?!?" she asked again.

"Well, the funny thing is, I'm not sure if we're actually *dating* dating. She sort of has a boyfriend, but we've gone out a few times together," James said.

"So, tell us everything," said Kelly, settling herself onto the bed, anticipating a long, sweet tale.

James told Sam and Kelly about Lauren, how they'd met, their first dinner together, "the other guy", all the time they've spent together. It was obvious to his friends that James was completely in love with her.

When they had settled into bed for the night, Sam and Kelly talked about James.

"I do believe that James is in love," said Kelly.

"I really wish that things will work out for him," Sam answered.

"Me too, he is such a nice guy. How is it that he never hooked up with anyone?"

"I don't know. I feel bad for him. It's strange, he has so many women friends, but he never seemed to find that someone who wanted him as more than a friend. For whatever reason, women never seemed to be interested in him, he gets turned down so often. The funny thing is, he is still friends with most of them; I don't know if I could handle that. It's one of the saddest things in life, you know, unrequited love. It's hard to talk about things like that with him. It gets both of us depressed."

"Well, if he gets together with Lauren, I think it would make up for some of the heartache that he has gone through," answered Kelly.

"Yes, I hope so."

"Can I come see you work some time?" Lauren asked James one day.

James was pleasantly surprised at her request. He was glad that she was interested in that part of his life, an aspect which he rarely discussed intimately with his friends or family. Although he dedicated much of his time and effort into his work life, James never considered work as important as everyday life. For him, work was work, although he knew that his work meant a lot more than an occupation to his patients. Work was not life, it was not what one lived for.

James asked Lauren if she would be interested in coming with him on an overnight shift. He was working next Friday night, which was typically pretty busy, the kind of shift which people envision when they think of the ER. She could borrow a pair of his scrubs and stay up with him all night.

Lauren was very excited about the idea. "It's a date!"

Lauren met James at his place on Friday. She brought an overnight bag with her. They were going to have lunch together, then they were going to get some sleep before leaving for the hospital. James and Lauren went to a Vietnamese place near where he lived, and they had a quiet lunch together. They were, by this time, perfectly comfortable spending time together without saying much. Conversation flowed effortlessly when they had something to say, but there was no longer any awkwardness when there was silence between them.

They headed back to James' place after lunch. James was accustomed to taking a long afternoon nap before his overnight shift. He read for about half an hour before he drifted off to sleep. It was more difficult for Lauren. She, like James, always felt a little sleepy after lunch, and they both loved the idea of siestas. It wasn't too hard to fall asleep, but she woke up after a couple of hours and couldn't go back to sleep again. She fidgeted around in the spare bedroom, reading a little, watching some television, but she found it impossible to get back to sleep. She laid there staring at the ceiling for a long time before she heard James' alarm clock go off.

James came to check if she was awake. She smiled at him as he peeked his head through the door. James asked her if she slept well, then he left her to take the first shower. He had a small dinner ready for them by the time she came out of the bathroom. It was some lasagna that he had pre-made and heated up. Lauren thought it was delicious. Italian food was great as leftovers, sometimes it was even better the second day. The twice-baked cheese was delectable.

It was already dark when they left. The drive was relatively quick. James worked at a municipal hospital on the outskirts of the city. It was a big nondescript looking building which stood quietly amid a residential neighborhood. The building wore a dusky facade which had faded slowly as the years wore on. Lauren could make out the outlines of the hospital grounds in the dark, dotted here and there with more nondescript buildings. James pulled into an outdoor lot adjacent to the hospital and parked the car. There were few cars in the lot at night, and there was no one walking about on the grounds. It seemed like they were the only two people within miles as they walked toward the hospital.

James led Lauren into the lobby and they disappeared through a series of nameless tiled corridors. Eventually the twists and turns led to a tiny locker room through which they entered. It was so close to the ER that she could hear the excited voices wafting down the hallway.

"You can change in there." James showed Lauren to a small bathroom and handed her a pair of scrubs. The bathroom was cramped but she managed to change into her costume for the night. The scrubs were a little baggy, but the fit wasn't too bad since James and she were pretty much the same height.

"I think we're ready to put you to work," said James when she emerged in her new attire.

"Sure, I'm ready to go!" she exclaimed.

James went into the bathroom and changed into his scrubs. When he returned to the small locker room, he took a bunch of stuff out of his backpack; index cards, a pen, something that looked like a cigarette lighter (it was his medical license stamp), a small pair of scissors, an ID, and a stethoscope. He took the stethoscope and draped it around Lauren's neck. "You can wear this tonight, I rarely need to use this thing."

The ER seemed to be overcrowded with sick people to Lauren, but according to James, it was relatively quiet. If this were quiet, she couldn't imagine what it would be like when it was busy. He said hello to some people as he made his way through the ER. He retrieved a piece of pink paper from a drawer full of papers and folded it into quarters. He noticed some people looking at an X-Ray that was displayed on a computer monitor. "That elbow is broken," he told them. "See that effusion?" James pointed to a seemingly random spot on the X-Ray. "He's got a type I radial head fracture, sling and Ortho." The people looking at the X-Ray acknowledged his comment and went back to their patient.

"Come with me, I have to take sign-out," he said to Lauren.

James walked over to a nurse and began talking to her. Lauren followed him hesitantly. He introduced them. "Lauren, this is Adrienne, one of the best doctors in the free world that money can't buy." The woman doctor, whom Lauren mistook as a nurse, laughed at James' introduction. "Adrienne, this is Lauren. She's one of my friends from med school. She's visiting from Philadelphia. She wanted to see what this crazy place was like."

"Good, good, welcome. Are you in Emergency Medicine?" Adrienne asked Lauren.

Lauren wasn't sure what she should say. Should she tell the truth and give James away? Maybe she'd get him in trouble if she told the truth.

"Uh, no, I take care of kids," she answered with the first plausible fabrication that popped into her head.

"Wow, that's great, I don't know how you do it. I have a couple of kids of my own and I can barely stand the two of them. I don't know how you handle all those crying kids everyday," said Adrienne.

"Yes, tell us, how *do* you take care of all those screaming babies?" James chimed in.

Lauren shot a quick dirty look at James. "Oh, it's not so bad, I managed all right," she answered with a barely perceptible tremor in her voice.

James snickered mischievously. Adrienne smiled, not sure what the joke was.

They walked through the ER methodically, stopping at each patient. Lauren could hardly understand what they were talking about most of the time. Much of their conversation consisted of medical terminology that she couldn't understand, but it seemed to her that Adrienne was telling James about the patients' illnesses. James jotted down a word or two onto his pink paper every now and then as Adrienne spoke, occasionally interjecting with a question. Thus they made their way around the ER in about ten minutes. Adrienne wished them goodnight and left them to the chatter of the Emergency Department.

James spent the next few minutes running around the ER, checking X-Rays, looking up tests in the computer, asking the nurses about some of the patients. Lauren felt a little self-conscious, adrift in the sea of patients, nurses, and doctors. Emergency Departments were small communities, and it was not difficult for those who worked there to spot those who did not belong to the ER, especially someone like Lauren, partly because she was a new face, partly because she was tall, and partly because she was so beautiful. Everyone noticed her, but they figured that she was ok when they saw James talking to her, and the scrubs helped keep her from being too conspicuous.

James settled down after his initial burst of activity. He was chatting with Lauren about how the ER was set up when one of the residents approached him to talk about a patient. It was a man with chest pain. James looked at his pink paper, apparently searching for some information on the patient. He asked the resident a couple of questions. What do you think about his story? Good or bad? Risk or no risk? What do you want to do with him? The resident thought it was best to admit the patient. James agreed with him, but added that "I would probably have sent him home, but I think your plan to admit him is fine, so let's do that."

After an hour, there was another change of doctors. The residents were changing shifts, James informed Lauren. We had a good team on tonight, he whispered to her. He introduced her to the new crew, whom they were going to spend the overnight with. There was Jessica, a pretty young woman who looked like she was still in high school; she was the senior resident working that night, and Gretchen and Elizabeth, who were the junior residents. Again, he introduced Lauren as his friend from medical school, now adding that she was a pediatrician.

After the residents changed shifts, James spoke to each resident and reviewed the cases with them. After an hour or so had passed by, the ER quieted down somewhat. He took Lauren with him and they walked around the ER together. This time, he spoke to Lauren about the patients in plain English. This guy was here with chest pain, there's probably nothing wrong with him, we were doing some tests to make sure everything was ok, he would be going home in a little bit. This woman was here for heart failure, see how her legs were all swollen, she's breathing a little fast, that's from having too much water in her body, we gave her some medicine to help her breathing, and she would need to stay in the hospital. It was a lot of information, but it was all very interesting to Lauren. She was amazed at what doctors were able to see and do.

They returned to the residents and James asked them if they wanted to talk about anything. Elizabeth asked him to talk about something called PE. They sat down together and then he gave a mini-lecture on this PE thing, again using words that Lauren didn't understand. The residents peppered him with questions, and he always had an answer for them.

As he was finishing up his talk, a young woman was brought into the ER by two paramedics. She was crying hysterically. James stood off to the side and listened to the paramedics tell Jessica about the patient. Lauren noticed that he was watching the patient from the corner of his eye.

Lauren overheard the conversation between Jessica and the paramedics. The young woman tried to overdose herself on some pills because her boyfriend broke up with her.

"Is she going to be all right?" asked Lauren.

"Yes, she'll be fine. I don't think she took anything serious," answered James.

"How can you tell?"

"A little from the story, a little from looking at her," he replied. "It's pretty easy to treat her from the medical side of things, but we'll never solve the bigger problem."

"What do you mean?"

"Boyfriend issues. He's probably a jerk, she can't let him go, stuff like that. We could never fix things like that. Sometimes they're better off going on a talk show."

"That's pretty cynical of you," Lauren said.

"Yes, I guess, it's easy to be cynical when we're not in their situation. Personally, I don't think I could ever understand why a woman would ever think of killing herself for a guy. No guy is worth that. And they're usually losers."

"This job, by the way, makes people cynical," James went on. "We see the worst side of people here, and it wears away your faith in human nature."

Lauren felt sadly for the young woman. She wished there was something she could do for her.

Jessica and Elizabeth were talking to the young woman. Jessica took some blood samples from the patient and Elizabeth did an EKG on her, then they gave the woman some ugly looking medicine (it was black!) to drink.

"So, are you going to be with us all night?" asked Jessica.

"Yes," answered Lauren, reminding herself that she was a pediatrician, and that she should act like a pediatrician, only she didn't know what that was.

"Great, well, welcome to our little corner of the world. Is this the first time you've been in an ER?"

"I was in an ER when I broke my arm when I was little. It was a little scary, but I don't remember it much."

"It must be certainly different from being a model."

"Yeah, it sure is." Lauren's voice hesitated for a second. "Actually, I'm a pediatrician."

"Oh, it's ok, you don't have to pretend anymore. James told us."

Lauren reddened. "I'm going to kill him!"

Jessica laughed. "Yeah, he's really a pain sometimes, but he's pretty funny."

Lauren looked around for James, he was talking to a patient.

"How long have you known each other?" asked Jessica.

"For a few months."

"How did you meet?" asked Jessica.

Lauren tells her "the story".

"Wow, that is so romantic! I hope you don't mind me saying this, but you guys make a great couple. Wouldn't it be amazing if everything works out? I'm really happy for you, and James is such a nice guy."

Lauren blushed again.

"Let me tell you a story," Jessica continued. "There was this one time when I was working with him overnight. The ER was packed, and we had a patient who had been in the waiting room for a long time. By the time we got him in to be examined it was pretty late at night, but he hadn't had anything to eat since lunch because he was waiting outside and had no money. The guy was starving. We went to look for some food for him but we had nothing left in the ER. I felt bad for him; but he was out of luck. I walked by later and saw him eating this big platter of food. I asked him where he got it, and he told me the other doctor got it for him. James went to the hospital cafeteria and bought dinner for the guy. That was so nice of him. He's always doing things like that, and he never mentions a word of it to anyone."

It was a touching story. Lauren thought how it was like James to do something like that.

James noticed them looking at him. He walked over.

"What's going on? What are you two talking about?" he asked them.

"Oh, nothing," answered Jessica. "Let me go see some patients. By the way, I want to be invited to the wedding," she remarked casually as she left James and Lauren together.

"*What* were you talking about?" James asked Lauren.

Lauren didn't answer him. At that moment, she was thinking that it wouldn't be half bad to be married to this wonderful man who was standing there so close to her. Yes, she could see them together. It *would* be rather nice, she thought.

Lauren began to feel a little tired by three in the morning. The doctors and nurses appeared to have inhuman stamina, it seemed to her. There was a break in the action and the five of them sat down and were chatting casually. Jessica asked Lauren about her travels, Elizabeth asked Lauren about what it was like working as a model, and Lauren asked them about medical school, the long hours, working nights. The conversation was interrupted by a commotion by the ER entrance. Everyone looked over. There was a man with a bloodstained shirt, leaning against the wall.

Before Lauren could react, the doctors scrambled out of their seats. The next few minutes were all a blur to Lauren. She watched the doctors from a few feet away, afraid of getting in anyone's way. James and Gretchen grabbed the guy and threw him onto a stretcher. Gretchen and Elizabeth put IVs into him. The nurses ran in and out of the room, retrieving medications and all sorts of equipment. They cut off the man's clothes. Jessica put a long tube into the man's mouth. Gretchen was squeezing blood into the patient through the IV. Someone came to do an X-Ray, and another person brought down more blood for the patient. They put another tube into the man's chest from which a lot of blood came out (was it supposed to do that?). More doctors came down to the ER, and they took the man to the Operating Room.

All of this took place in about fifteen minutes.

"Good job, guys," said James as he went around patting the residents on their backs. They sat back down and reviewed the case; what they did right, what they could have done better, why the man had to go to the OR, and something about keeping patients' blood pressures low that Lauren didn't understand, and that James said was controversial. James then went over the whole thing with Lauren. The way he looked when he came in, that was a look of death, he told her. That's what people look like when they were going to die. He had a stab wound to his right chest, and he wasn't breathing right. Jessica put the tube into his mouth to breathe for him. The IVs were put in to replace the blood loss from his stab wound. The X-Ray showed that he was bleeding into his lung from the stab wound, and they had to put in the chest tube to fix the problem. He had to have an emergent operation because he was bleeding too much from his lung.

The rest of the night remained uneventful, much to the delight of the doctors. Even more satisfying was the news from the OR that the patient had made it. James congratulated the residents on a successful save.

In the morning, a new doctor came in and took sign-out from James, repeating the walk around the ER that they took twelve hours ago. Lauren was tired and fell asleep in the car as James drove them home. He made her eat a little cereal before putting her to bed. She was so tired that she barely had the energy to change out of the scrubs. She collapsed onto the bed and fell asleep immediately.

Lauren slept soundly. Staying up all night wears down the body, even if she wasn't doing any work in particular. She woke up at a little past three in the afternoon. There was a ray of sunlight peeking through a corner in the window blinds. At first she wasn't sure where she was, she was not in her bed. She laid there and collected her thoughts. She was at James' place. She was at the hospital last night. She wondered what time it was. There was still sunlight outside. She rose slowly and stretched. A yawn escaped from her lips. The apartment was silent. James must be still sleeping. She slowly realized that she was rather hungry. What was there to eat in the apartment? She didn't know.

She looked at her watch to check the time. It was later than she thought. She pulled back the blinds and looked outside. It was sunny. She saw people in the streets, perhaps running errands, perhaps enjoying the pleasant weather. In the darkened room, she had been oblivious to the vibrant energy of the world that went on all day without her. She did not miss it; she was too tired.

Lauren walked to the bathroom quietly, not wanting to wake up James. She washed her face and brushed her teeth. The cold water refreshed her spirits, she felt she was slowly recuperating from her fatigue. She toweled her face dry and walked into the living room. James' bedroom door was half-closed; he was probably still sleeping. There was a note and a sandwich on a plate on the dining table. James wrote that he had lunch earlier while she was still sleeping. He made an extra sandwich for her. There was milk, orange juice, soda in the fridge. There were potato chips on the kitchen counter. She should help herself. He would probably wake up around four or five, but she could wake him up anytime if she needed something.

She poured herself a glass of milk and sat down at the table. She smiled when she looked at the plate that James left for her. There were two sandwiches cut in halves, with lettuce, tomato slices, and a dollop of dijon mustard on the side. It was the kind of lunch that moms made for their kids. She thought it very cute and very thoughtful.

Lauren sat in the living room and read after lunch. She had brought a book with her. She read for about an hour or so before she heard James stir in his bedroom. In a few minutes he emerged from his bedroom, hair astray, a little groggy, but a smile lit up his face when he saw Lauren sitting on the sofa.

"Good morning." He looked at the book she was reading. "*Emma*. Great book. I love Jane Austen."

They spoke about the overnight at dinner.

"It was pretty sad to see someone try to end their life," Lauren said.

"Yes. Unfortunately it happens all too often. On the other hand, it's not as bleak as it seems sometimes. Fortunately, most people aren't serious about killing themselves, and even then, most people don't do it right. Personally, I'd feel rather embarrassed if I tried to kill myself and somehow screwed it up."

"Taking pills is a horrible way to die," James went on. "It's rarely successful, and when it is successful, it is usually a long and painful death."

"Is there such a thing as a *good* way to die?"

James pondered the question for a moment.

"Carbon monoxide. Painless, pretty sure bet, if you take the necessary precautions."

Lauren thought James was being rather morbid. She changed the subject.

Despite the distressing moments involving the suicidal young woman, Lauren enjoyed the time she spent in the ER with James. It was very enlightening, seeing the ER from a doctor's point of view. She was glad that James took the time to go over everything with her; it made her feel more involved; she wasn't just a casual observer. It was nice to see James at work. It was obvious that everyone, particularly the residents, loved working with him. She always knew that he was a kind and caring doctor, and she was glad that she was able to see this for herself. He was what she always thought him to be.

Lauren asked James to have dinner with her that weekend. Andrea and Peter would be joining them, she told him. James was excited at the prospect of meeting her friends. Despite all the time that they had spent together recently, they had yet to meet the important people in each other's circles.

Lauren wanted to have a nice dinner with her closest friends, something special. She arranged to get reservations at one of the more extravagant restaurants in the city. There were perks to working for an elite modeling agency, and every once in a while Lauren made use of the connections that were available to her, even though she always felt a little guilty at being treated differently from everyone else.

James was the first to arrive at the restaurant. He checked his watch, but he already knew that he was a little early as usual. He ordered a ginger ale while he waited at the bar, pretending to be comfortable, hoping to see Lauren soon. There were a few other parties there, having drinks at the bar, probably waiting as well. The voices were kept low, talk of vacations, children, and mutual friends. James was skimming over the menu when he noticed a hush in the hovering conversations. He looked up. It was Lauren.

She was simply stunning. It seemed like everyone became speechless when she walked through the door. It was impossible for anyone there not to notice her. Lauren wore her favorite black dress, a long, strapless model which clinged tightly to her lissome body. The top was modest, but the skirt was cut very high, drawing covetous glances from the men and envious glares from some women. She wore her hair up for the occasion, but her makeup was simple and modest. She was something extraordinary, and everyone there knew it.

She smiled gaily when she spotted James. Lauren made her way through the crowd to him, shunning the admiring looks which surrounded her. Everyone turned to see the lucky guy that she had come to meet. Lauren knew that she had drawn everyone's attention, and she decided to be a little bit mischievous. She walked up to James and gave him a peck on the cheek. "I missed you so much, honey," she announced audibly, then she pulled James to her by his tie and kissed him passionately in front of her audience. James was so surprised that he didn't even know how to respond. She took the breath out of him. He just froze there as Lauren drew her lips over his and kissed him seductively.

James was still a little dazed as Lauren whispered in his ear. "I just wanted to give them a little show," she giggled softly.

It took James a couple of minutes and a couple of sips of ginger ale before he could collect himself. Lauren was still smiling brightly when he focused his eyes on her.

"Look at this! A suit and a tie. I feel honored," she said. Lauren knew that James didn't like dressing up in suits and ties. "You look great."

"I think I'm the one who should be honored after that kiss," James laughed.

"I hope you enjoyed it."

James smiled shyly. "Now you, you look wonderful. I've never seen you wear your hair up before. It looks great. I love it."

Lauren was used to compliments, but there was a certain heartfelt sincerity in his words which made his compliments special to her.

"Are those new earrings? That dress looks terrific on you. I think I'm the envy of every man here."

Lauren smiled with self-satisfaction. She knew that she looked good, and she was pleased that he had noticed. She even blushed a little.

Lauren didn't want to sit at the bar amidst the furtive glances that surrounded her. She asked James if he would mind if they waited at the table inside. James was fine with the idea, but he wasn't sure if they would be seated; they were still early for their reservation and not everyone was there. Lauren told him that it shouldn't be a problem. She walked over to the maitre d' who met her with a warm smile and greeted her by name. They spoke for a few seconds. Lauren waved James over and the maitre d' escorted them into the dining room.

"We're all set," she beamed. Lauren wrapped her arm around James' and snuggled close to him as they went into the restaurant. James caught a scent of Lauren's soft perfume as they walked together. It would remind him of her, of this night, forever. He was oblivious to the eyes that followed them as they crossed the dining room to their table. The attention that they drew from the other diners went unnoticed. His thoughts were of Lauren, and Lauren alone. She ordered a bottle of white wine while they waited for Andrea and Peter. They talked and laughed like old friends. No, they were more like two lovers, entirely engulfed in one another. The outside world did not exist to them. They had no need for it; they had each other.

Times like these were exquisite and flawless. Times like these were meant to be cherished. Neither Lauren nor James thought about where they were in their relationship, or where they were going. Were they merely platonic friends? Were they significant others? Were they lovers? Yes, there were feelings there, although they have not made love physically. They had certainly made love to each other in many other ways, in the secret smiles they shared, in the yearning that radiated from their eyes, and in the love they expressed for each other in unspoken words. There were no questions or hesitations that night. Lauren remembered how handsome James looked, how kind he was, how he met her every wish, every desire. James remembered the happiness he felt in just being with her, laughing at her great sense of humor, sharing in her glow, floating in the love that she offered to him. No, there was no nervous anticipation of the night ahead, there would be no need for that.

Lauren and James were finishing the bottle of wine when Andrea and Peter arrived. They found Lauren and James sitting at their table as they came into the restaurant. Lauren was completely absorbed in something that James was saying. Her body language showed that there was something more in their relationship than Andrea had realized; the way she tilted her head toward James when she listened to him, the twinkle in her eyes as she looked at him, the arch of her eyebrows as she smiled. Then she was laughing softly, playfully hitting him on his arm. She beckoned him to come closer to her so that she could speak to him secretively. She touched his face endearingly as she whispered in his ear. His face reflected delightfully as she spoke to him. They were happy; it was easy to see.

"I don't think they would miss us if we didn't show up," Peter said to Andrea.

"I think you're right," she answered.

They approached the two lovers unnoticed until they were practically standing next to them. Lauren greeted them enthusiastically, excessively. She caressed James behind his neck and pecked him on the cheek as she introduced him to her friends.

"Nice to finally meet you," James smiled, as Lauren wiped a remnant of her lipstick from his cheek with a dampened napkin.

Dinner went off superbly. Perhaps it was the wine, perhaps it was the company, perhaps it was Lauren, but James was not his usual timid self that night. There was no trace of the diffidence that he characteristically displayed when he met new people. He was talkative and carefree, and he hit it off with Andrea and Peter. Lauren was overjoyed to see her closest friends get along so swimmingly.

When James excused himself from the table, Lauren had the chance to talk to Andrea and Peter alone.

"Well?" she asked.

"I like him," Andrea answered.

"Two thumbs up," Peter echoed.

"I think he's in love with you," said Andrea.

"Definitely," Peter chimed in.

Lauren smiled demurely. She didn't say a word. She was inwardly delighted that her friends confirmed what she had always known, but which she had never allowed herself to recognize. She knew that he had wanted to be more than friends. She knew that it was more than a fleeting crush. Tonight, she realized that it was what she wanted as well; she wanted James to be in love with her. She was a little in love with him too.

Lauren had never admitted as much to herself, but she had mixed feelings about her relationship with James. She knew that James was interested in her. There was no question about that, but she was ambivalent about taking that next step with him. It wasn't that she was unsure of James as a person. She knew that he was funny, he was kind, he was a good friend. She knew that he would be just as tenderhearted as her lover, his feelings and his character were genuine. He would be true, he would never do anything to hurt her, he would love her. On the other hand, she never felt the type of physical attraction that formed most of her relationships. He was rather quiet now and then, he was hard to read at times. She loved him as a friend, to be sure, but did she have feelings for him beyond that?

It bothered Lauren that she never felt that overpowering physical attraction toward James. She didn't know herself whether that had kept her from pursuing him as a boyfriend in the first place. She didn't know which was worse, that she didn't feel an overwhelming physical attraction toward him, or that physical attraction had kept her from forming an engagement with someone she liked. She was ashamed of herself at the prospect of the latter. It made her superficial. She was no better than any of those men who wanted to sleep with her because of her looks. She should be better than that.

Lauren often talked to Andrea about her relationships. In the course of their conversations, Lauren realized that she had never really had a serious long-term relationship. She had never been in a relationship where there was talk about the rest of their lives. Perhaps even, she had never been in love.

"How do you know?" Lauren asked.

Andrea laughed.

"I don't know. I don't think there's a simple answer. It's probably different for different people."

Andrea asked Lauren some rather trite questions about her feelings toward James.

"Do you think about him all the time?" No. Yes. Maybe. No.

"Do you miss him when he's gone?" Yes, most definitely.

"Is he the first person you think about after you wake up? Is he the last person you think about before you fall asleep?" Yes, sometimes.

"Do you prefer him to any other man?" I don't know.

"Can you see the two of you in bed together?" Yes.

"Can you see the two of you having children together?" Yes.

"Can you see the two of you growing old together?" Yes.

"Do you love him?"

"How did you know that Peter was the one?" Lauren asked. She had never asked Andrea this question before.

"I can't explain it, I just knew. He felt right. After we had been together for a short time, we both felt that we were meant to be with each other."

The discussion could have gone on forever, and they still wouldn't be able to grasp the elusive substance that they were trying to define.

Lauren didn't know what she wanted, at least, not until that night. Seeing James at the bar, in his suit and tie, he looked more handsome than ever. He was waiting for her, and she felt a gladness in her heart knowing that he was waiting for her. Suddenly, she saw him in a different light. She felt that she wanted to be with him, she needed him, she loved him. She had never felt so strongly about anyone. There was a fierce, profound desire to be with him. She had never kissed anyone with so much intensity, with so much love, with so much abandon, as when she kissed James that evening.

Once she committed herself, Lauren could not help herself from falling further. She was suddenly thrust into a time and place that was foreign to her. She felt excited, dizzy, vulnerable, ecstatic, peaceful, protected, beloved, all at the same time. Lauren looked at James with adoring eyes. She wanted to hold him, to kiss him, to feel his body against hers. She held James endearingly as they entered the restaurant as one. She basked in his warmth. She was happy being with this wonderful man, she was happy to be his. Suddenly, James seemed perfect.

Dinner was delightful. Andrea and Peter turned in for the night afterward, leaving the two lovers to themselves. Lauren and James walked around aimlessly for a little while, looking at store windows, wandering in the moonlit night, holding hands lovingly.

"I have an idea," James said abruptly.

He flagged down a taxicab and escorted Lauren into the waiting car. He whispered the directions to the driver, who dutifully remained silent about their destination. Lauren was intrigued.

"Where are you taking me?" she inquired. She rested her head on his shoulder, her hair tickling the soft skin on his cheek. She petted the back of his hand softly as she spoke to him.

"You'll see," he said quietly. Her sparkling eyes met his smile as he turned toward her. Her face was filled with a joyful expression as she gazed up at him. It was a look which would have captured anyone's heart.

The cab made its way crosstown. Lauren watched the streetlights pass by, hardly paying attention to where they were going. She was content to rest in James' arms and let him take her where he may.

The taxi pulled up and stopped in front of what looked like an office building. Lauren couldn't make out where they were through the foggy windows. James paid the driver and helped her out of the cab. They were at one of the city's landmark skyscrapers.

James and Lauren caught the last elevator up to the observatory at the top of the building. It was late, and there were only a few people left.

Lauren scurried excitedly to the edge of the observatory. She held onto the railing and looked down all around her. "I've never been up here at night," she told him. "It's beautiful." The air was a little cold as the night breeze swirled around her. James came up behind her and placed his arms around her, warming her in his embrace. He kissed her gently behind her ear and nuzzled her neck softly. She settled herself comfortably in his arms, nestling against his body, and they watched the city night together, dreaming of things that were closer at hand.

Time passed by all too quickly. An attendant made his way around the observatory, announcing that it was closing time. James was reluctant to let go of Lauren, and Lauren was reluctant to be let go. Lauren pirouetted herself about so that they were face to face. Wordlessly, they brought their lips together. It was a long, delicate kiss, a kiss between two friends as they became lovers, a kiss between two lovers who surrendered to each other.

Lauren asked James to come home with her. They held each other tenderly during the short ride to her place, resting softly against each other in the taxi. She kissed him again as soon as they entered her apartment. Their faces were full of feeling as they looked at each other. Lauren skipped ahead into the apartment and retrieved a bottle of Chardonnay from a small cabinet. She handed James the wine and asked him to fill the glasses. The apartment was dimly lit by a single light from a lamp in a corner. Lauren found a lighter and lit some candles that were scattered around the living room. A scent mixed of lilacs, vanilla, and berries slowly cascaded through the apartment. Lauren turned on the stereo and a slow jazz melody began to fill the room. James walked into the living room with the wineglasses and the two friends toasted each other silently. Lauren took the glasses from James and set them down on a coffee table. She smiled seductively and kissed him again. She pressed her body to his and they began to sway to the soulful music, dancing slowly in the candlelight.

"This is wonderful," James whispered.

Lauren answered him with a soft kiss. She laid her head on his shoulder and pulled him ever closer to her, their bodies melting together into one.

They could have danced forever, but the night and the music wore on. Lauren asked James to refill their glasses while she changed out of her dress. In a few moments, Lauren returned in a pair of silk pajamas consisting of a demure, lacy camisole and a pair of modest length shorts. She handed James a T-shirt and a pair of pajama pants that she thought he might fit into. James handed her a glass of wine and changed into her sleepwear. The pajamas fit him surprisingly well, and Lauren smiled with delight as he rejoined her in the candlelight. They snuggled up to each other on the sofa and slowly finished the wine, sharing their thoughts, drinking in each other. It was deep in the night when the two lovers retired to her bed. They spent the night adrift in sensual caresses and tender kisses. It was almost morning when they fell asleep, Lauren cuddled in James' arms.

James and Lauren became a couple after that night. Lauren felt that she had never been so happy. For the first time in her life, she was sharing her life with someone who truly loved her. It was a wonderful feeling being with someone you loved. She even enjoyed the minor inconveniences that came with the relationship. She liked running into him in the bathroom in the morning. She liked checking in with James before accepting invitations to social engagements. She liked calling James when she ran late. She always told him to have dinner without her, but he always waited for her, no matter how late the hour was.

Of course, life with James was more than blissful inconveniences. It was great to have a nice homemade dinner waiting for her when she came home from classes. It was nice to get backrubs when she was tired. It was even nice to return the favor when James needed some pampering after a long day. She liked helping him shop for clothes. She liked exploring together, trying new restaurants, discovering new places in the surrounding country, finding special ways to surprise and delight one another. They were on a honeymoon of sorts, but neither of them had realized it.

Lauren and James were practically living together during this time. They didn't exactly talk about moving in together, it just sort of slowly happened. They exchanged keys a couple of days after they spent that first night together. They spent most of their time at Lauren's, unless James was working late. At other times, Lauren and James spent the day at his place, and she would stay with him overnight. There were days when their schedules didn't work out; sometimes she had an early shoot in the morning, sometimes he had to work an overnight shift, so occasionally they spent a night apart, but they always spoke to each other everyday, and rarely did a day go by when they didn't see each other.

They lived like husband and wife, yet they never consummated their relationship physically. Lauren and James slept together every night, but they didn't "sleep together". It was a rather unusual living situation, Andrea thought. As intimate as they were with each other, Lauren and James never talked about it, and perhaps, neither of them considered it. It was as if an unspoken agreement was formed between them.

Lauren was a little surprised that James never pressured her to have sex. It was clear that all of the men that she had dated in the past, like Brian, wanted to get her into bed more than anything else. Now here was a man with whom she shared her bed every night, and yet he never made a move on her. In a way, this made her feel that James was even more special, particularly since she had already decided that she was ready to be with him if he ever so desired. The situation was confusing at first. Lauren always thought that a perfect relationship necessitated a perfect sex partner. She was surprised to feel that their relationship was quite perfect even without the physical act of sex. They expressed their physical love for each other in different ways, and she was perfectly happy with the way things were. She was in no hurry, she had never been in a hurry. She felt the time will come.

James, for his part, had always wanted to be with Lauren, but he didn't want it to be a short term affair. He had that chance before. It wasn't that he wanted to save himself until marriage, he was not so old-fashioned. He wanted more than a physical relationship from Lauren, he wanted her heart and soul. He wanted her to be his forever before they made love together. Sexual pleasure was good for a few hours, but love was for a lifetime. It would be too painful if their intimate relationship did not outlast their sexual relationship. He would miss her too much.

And so Lauren and James went on.

Lauren's parents came to visit her one weekend that winter. They were going to see a play and maybe go to one of the museums. James figured that he wouldn't see Lauren that weekend, so he was surprised when she asked him to have dinner with her parents.

James believed that one of the best ways to a woman's heart was through her family, so he always made an effort to win over the relatives of the woman that he was interested in; parents, siblings, pets, and everyone else that was important to that special someone. As it turned out, he didn't really need to make much of an effort in this case, Lauren's parents were already predisposed to liking him.

Lauren and James had gone to a concert with her younger sister, Michelle, a few weeks before, and Michelle really liked him. He was funny, he was genuine, he was nice, but most importantly, she could see how much he cared for Lauren, and how happy her sister was when they were together. Michelle gave a glowing report to her parents, who normally tried not to be too inquisitive of their daughters' personal lives, but they couldn't help being pleased that Lauren was in a happy relationship. Lauren had mentioned James to her parents before, but she never told them that they were dating. It seemed, according to Michelle's account, that they had been together for a long while already, and a spark of interest grew around James. They wanted to meet James for themselves, but they felt a little uncomfortable asking Lauren to introduce him to them. After all, her parents did not know how close they were in their relationship.

Lauren spared her parents from anticipation. She wanted them to meet James. She wanted James to meet them. She phoned her parents and told them that she was going to bring a friend of hers to dinner. Mrs. Corvo, of course, understood that she meant James, and she was happy at the prospect of meeting him. Lauren's dad, forgetting himself, asked her who she was going to bring.

"He's a good friend of mine. His name is James," she told her father.

"Oh, James. So we're finally going to meet him," he answered.

His wife gave him a little nudge. "What?!? What did I say?" he asked her, holding his hand over the telephone receiver.

Lauren thought it was funny that her parents wanted to meet James so badly. She knew that she had never told her parents that they were dating, but now it seemed they had caught on. Michelle probably told them, she figured. Whenever she spoke of James to her parents, she described him as her friend. He was the friend who taught her how to make tofu stir-fry, the friend who went biking with her in the fall, her friend who she could always depend on. She didn't tell her parents that she was living with James, that she was sharing her bed with him. She wondered how her parents would react if they knew.

Lauren went to a matinee with her parents, then they went shopping for a few hours, seeing the sights of the city. James was to meet them at the restaurant later that evening. He knew that he had to be prepared for a little bit of an inspection, so he spent a little extra time scrutinizing his appearance in the apartment. Was the tie on straight? Was it too long? He couldn't get it to dimple right the first time. Maybe a different pair of shoes. He hadn't been so meticulous about his appearance since his date with Lauren at the boat basin. He was a little more nervous about meeting her parents than meeting her, because, after all, he had already known her before their first date.

Lauren and her parents were waiting for him when he arrived. He shook their hands warmly and told them how pleased he was to meet them.

James was a little nervous at first, but Lauren's parents liked him for his polite manners, the warmth in which he treated their daughter, and the undisguised delight they saw in their daughter's eyes when she spoke of him. Of course, they liked the fact that he was a doctor, and Lauren's father couldn't help himself from interrogating James about his work in the ER. He was surprised when Lauren told them that she tagged along with James one night. "It was amazing," she beamed, "and *he*, is a wonderful doctor." James was a little embarrassed by the compliment, but he liked that she spoke so highly of him in front of her parents.

If there was a test, James passed it. Lauren could sense that her parents approved of James, not that she would admit to her looking for their stamp of approval. Nevertheless, she was rather pleased that her parents took a liking to James. After dinner, Lauren was to return to the hotel with her parents. To her surprise, Lauren's father asked James to come along with them. James declined politely. "I think she wants to spend some time alone with you," he told them. "It was great meeting you, I hope you have a great stay." James shook their hands again and wished them a goodnight.

As James turned to take his leave, Lauren ran up to him and gave him a big hug.

"Thanks for coming out tonight," she said, "I love you." Then she kissed him on the cheek before returning to her parents.

He was still awake when the telephone rang around midnight.

"Hi sweetie," came the familiar voice on the line.

"How was the rest of the night? I hope your parents had a good time."

"We had fun. I was really glad to see them." Lauren told James about her day with her parents. Everybody enjoyed the play, the music was great, there were a couple of spectacular dance numbers. She bought a necklace for her mother at Paul G. Her mom thought it was too expensive but Lauren talked her into accepting the gift. Her dad liked Lombardi's, but he was good and refrained from buying too many sweets. They had a nightcap at the hotel bar. They talked about him a little. James pretended not to be curious about what they said about him, but Lauren knew that he was interested. She teased him a little, not letting James know what her parents thought of him. Finally she relented. "They loved you."

"I miss you," he told her. It was the first time in many weeks that they did not spend the night together.

"I miss you, too." She meant it. It felt strange not to have James in bed with her. She felt empty in an odd way. He felt it too.

"See you tomorrow night?" he asked. Lauren's parents were heading back home in the afternoon.

"Yes, I'll miss you until then," she found herself repeating the same sentiment. "Goodnight. I love you."

"Goodnight. Love you too."

Lauren was invited to a wedding, and she asked James to accompany her. Actually, they were at that point of a relationship where she really didn't need to ask him. It was understood. She had a wedding to go to, therefore he was to go with her.

The bride was a friend of Lauren's from the modeling agency. Consequently, there were many people from the agency at the wedding, including many of the models. James remarked that he had never seen a wedding where there were so many beautiful people. Lauren saw these people all the time at work, so to her they were nothing extraordinary.

James was always a little uncomfortable at parties, especially when he didn't know anybody, and this wedding was no exception. The only person he knew there was Lauren, so he was a bit clingy at the reception. Lauren felt a little sorry for his social anxiety, but it was sort of cute in a way. She introduced him to her friends as they mingled among the crowd. "This is my current boy toy," she joked, causing her friends to chuckle appreciatively.

James made the rounds with Lauren a couple of times before she left him to chat with a close friend. "I'll be right back," she told him. It was awkward sitting alone at the table, so he got up to get a drink. He felt more comfortable with a drink in his hand, it made him feel like he was doing something, even if it was just holding a drink.

James asked the bartender for a whiskey and ginger ale.

"Interesting drink," a feminine voice commented from behind.

James turned to see who made the remark. It came from a tall blonde who stood behind him at the bar. She was very attractive; she must be a model, he thought.

The blonde sidled beside him. "I'll have the same," she told the bartender.

"Hi, I'm Danielle," she introduced herself. She held out her hand for James. When they shook hands, she pressed his hand in a meaningful way, but her subtle message did not register with James.

"Bride or groom?" she asked. James told her he was with someone who knew the bride. Danielle knew that he was there with Lauren. She saw them come in together.

Danielle made small talk with James. She was very flattering towards him. You must be really smart to be a doctor, I really admire doctors. You are so cute, and such a nice guy too. You look like you take pretty good care of yourself, what do you do to keep in shape? Lauren was so lucky to find a guy like you.

Danielle was flirtatious in more than words. She touched him softly here and there as she peppered him with compliments. She caressed his shoulder seductively as she went on about his physique. She held his fingers suggestively as she admired his soft hands.

Danielle's practiced coquetry was not lost on James. He wondered that she should be coming on to him, when she knew that he was there with Lauren. Perhaps it was only his imagination, he thought, perhaps she was being friendly, perhaps she was like that with everyone.

The DJ began playing a mix of dance club favorites as the party guests moved onto the dance floor. "I love this song, come dance with me," she said to James. Danielle took James' drink and placed it on the bar. She kissed him on the cheek and grabbed him by the hand, leading her reluctant partner to the dance floor.

Lauren was still chatting with her friend when she noticed that James was talking to Danielle. Danielle had an infamous reputation at the agency. She had a habit of sleeping around, and had a penchant for other women's husbands and boyfriends. She made it no secret that she liked the thrill of seducing someone else's lover. She enjoyed insinuating herself into other people's relationships, it made her feel sexy and powerful. She would seduce the man, break up the relationship, then dump him. They were meaningless to her once she had her use of them. She was remorseless at the heartache that she caused. It was the man's fault, not hers, she was innocent. There were a lot of hard feelings toward her at the agency. She would have been asked to leave if not for the fact that she brought in a lot of money to the agency.

Lauren saw that Danielle was openly flirting with James. Her initial instinct was to run over and escort James away from Danielle. For the first time in her life, she felt threatened by another woman. Suddenly she felt extremely possessive of James. Lauren was indignant at Danielle's audacity, she was practically all over him, and Lauren was getting a little incensed watching them go on. She was about to cross the room when she saw them step onto the dance floor. A quick tempo'd hip-hop number was playing at the time, and Lauren stopped and watched them spin and twirl to the fast moving rhythm. The DJ changed gears at the end of the song and slipped into a slow ballad. James was about to step off the floor but Danielle stopped him. She embraced him tightly as they swayed to the soft music. Danielle became bolder and bolder as they danced together. She pulled James to her tightly, grinding her hips against his yielding body. From where Lauren was watching them, James seemed to be enjoying himself. Lauren was very upset, overrun by feelings of betrayal, jealousy, and anger. He seemed to have forgotten about her completely, and then, she saw Danielle try to kiss him. James pulled away from her and whispered something to her. There was a puzzled look on Danielle's face, followed by a look of irritation. She said something to him in return, and James answered her parry softly. They finished the dance together, but they were no longer flesh against flesh. Lauren wondered what he said to her. They stepped off the dance floor when the song ended. James said a few words to Danielle, and they went their separate ways.

Lauren's heart lightened, and she almost smiled. She always knew that he would be true to her. She had no reason to feel so angry and jealous, she told herself. She saw James walking around the reception, obviously looking for her among the guests. Lauren snuck up behind him and tapped him on the shoulder. He was so relieved to see her, she could see it in his face. "Boy, am I glad to see you. Please don't leave me alone again." James told her about his misadventure with Danielle. She was glad that he told her everything, that he didn't try to hide anything from her.

The rest of the wedding was uneventful until the last dance. James and Lauren were swaying cheek to cheek to an old love song.

"Maybe this will be us someday," he whispered.

Lauren was silent. The words shook her. It could happen. It could be real. It would be a big step in their relationship. It would be a big step in her life. An unexpected, odd feeling came over her; an uncertain, uneasy sensation that made her fearful.

Lauren was genuinely affected. She rued over those words constantly in her mind. Lauren had never seriously thought about marriage. Ever. With anyone. The prospect was unsettling. She loved him, she wanted to be with him, she hoped to make love to him, but was she ready to marry him? Was she ready to settle down? Was she ready to spend the rest of her life with him? Was she ready to start a family?

She honestly believed that they knew each other as well as two people could ever get to know each other. They knew each other as well as they knew themselves, but she also said to herself that they had been together only for a few months. James had always hinted that he wanted to be with her, but she didn't understand that he meant forever. Now she knew.

Lauren didn't realize it, but she was afraid making such a commitment. She had never been in a relationship with someone like James before. She had never dated anyone who wanted her heart more than her body. In a way, he was exactly what she was searching for, someone who cared for her, someone who was true, someone who would be there for her no matter what. She had been hurt many times before Brian, and she was afraid of getting hurt again. As unlikely as it seemed, it was possible for James to hurt her. If he hurt her now, the pain would be terrible, but if she engaged her heart to him, the pain would be devastating. How could she allow herself to be so vulnerable, to leave her heart and soul at the mercy of another?

James, for his part, was perfectly ready to spend the rest of his life with Lauren. She was someone special, she was everything that he had been looking for. The only reason that kept him from proposing was that he thought Lauren needed more time. He understood that they had been together only for a short time, and that she was probably not ready to make such a commitment. He loved her, and he would wait for her as long as she wished.

Lauren did not like being so unsure of herself. She didn't know what she wanted. She loved James, she could at least admit that much to herself. He felt so right in so many ways, but she was also fearful. She was afraid of giving herself completely, but she was also afraid of losing him because she couldn't make such a commitment.

The insecurity, the fear of the unknown began to put a strain on Lauren. She transferred her internal struggle into an unconscious desire to separate herself from James. By breaking up with him, she would resolve the conflict that raged inside her. She became ever so critical of James, not so much in words as in thought. She didn't like the way he dressed, she didn't like his work hours, sharing the bathroom became a nuisance, he was too quiet, his jokes were out of place. The relationship was not working for her, at least it was so in her mind.

Lauren did not need to express her feelings in words. James felt Lauren distancing herself from him. Ever so slowly, all the little things that he had cherished dissipated; the way that she crept up behind him and kissed him when he was cooking, the way that she looked at him as they laid in bed talking, the way that she held onto him when they walked about in the park. Gone were the soft caresses, the gentle whispers, the wordless expressions of love. Their kisses became mechanical. She stole away the spontaneity and the passion of their relationship.

As conflicted as Lauren's feelings were, she found it impossible to talk to James about it. She could talk to James about anything else, about things that she would never talk about with anyone else, but she couldn't talk to him about their relationship, perhaps the one thing that was most important to them both. She was afraid that she may say things that she would regret if she aired her feelings. It was one thing if she turned him down when he wanted to spend the night with her, it was quite another thing to turn him down when he wanted to spend his life with her.

Things could not continue the way it was.

James didn't understand what was happening. He knew something was wrong. He wasn't sure if she was angry with him over Danielle, or whether there was something else going on. He knew Lauren well enough to know that she could be a little hostile when she became stressed, but this was something quite different. It almost seemed that she was purposefully making things difficult. She was even cold to him sometimes, which she had never been before.

"Lauren, can we talk?" he asked her one night after they had dinner at her place.

"About what?" she turned on the television.

James sat down beside her. He asked her to turn off the television.

Lauren felt nervous and uncomfortable. She wanted to escape somehow. She didn't want to talk about this.

"I want to talk about us," James continued.

"What do you mean?"

"Is something wrong? You seemed upset with me the last couple of weeks. Are you mad at me? Did I do something?"

"No, nothing's wrong," she lied. "I'm not mad at you."

"You just seem ... sort of distant."

Lauren reassured him that everything was fine.

James went on.

"Lauren, are you okay with where we're going in this relationship?"

Lauren was silent.

"I think you know that I want to be with you, not for days or months, but forever. Do you see the two of us being together?"

James searched Lauren's face intently. Her expression was filled with doubt and hesitation; he had his answer. Lauren realized that he saw through her, he felt what she felt. She looked away from him, she couldn't face him.

"James ..." she said. There was no turning back. "James, I don't know, maybe we should break things off for a bit. I think I need some time to myself."

He didn't say a word, he already knew this was coming. It was still painful nevertheless.

The two friends were silent. He wanted to ask her if she wanted a temporary break or a permanent separation. He didn't pose the question. He didn't want to know the answer. Perhaps he knew what she was going to say.

"Are you sure?" James broke the silence.

"Yes. I've been thinking it over." She lied, she wasn't sure at all, not even for a second.

James was surprisingly calm. He was prepared to give her as much time as she wanted, but he realized then that she may never want him to come back to her.

Nothing more was said. Nothing more was done. James rose from the sofa and took his jacket from her closet. He returned to Lauren. He wanted to give her a kiss goodnight, perhaps a kiss goodbye, but he thought that she wouldn't want him to do that. He was mistaken. James touched Lauren gently on her shoulder. She looked up. "I'll come pick up my stuff in the morning, is that okay?" Lauren nodded in reply.

Lauren began to cry as soon as James closed the door behind him. She didn't know exactly why she was crying. She didn't know exactly what was wrong. She didn't know why she was feeling the way that she was. After all, she got what she wanted, didn't she?

Unbeknownst to her, James shared in her tears as well. Unheard tears ran softly down his face as he walked out of Lauren's apartment. It was a long, cold walk home. His dream was over.

"Maybe this will be us someday." The words seemed so innocuous.

James was resigned to Lauren's feelings. He retrieved his belongings from Lauren's place the next day. He felt incredibly sad as he left his key on her end table. He looked around the apartment, perhaps he was seeing it for the last time.

Lauren stayed away from the apartment as James gathered his things. She could not bear to see him. It was painful enough as it was.

James and Lauren kept in touch even after the breakup, and in a strange way, they remained good friends. Their friendship was weakened by the loss of their romantic relationship, but the strength of the friendship from which they formed their love for each other was more than enough to keep them together. They both felt hurt, but they didn't blame each other. They still thought of each other, they still respected each other's feelings, and they still loved each other, though perhaps in a different way. Most of all, they did not want to lose the wonderfully intimate friend that they had found.

A few weeks passed by. James' phone rang innocently one morning. It was Lauren's sister.

"Hi James, it's Michelle. I'm over at Lauren's place. Listen, she got into a bad accident in Paris. No, she's ok, I mean, we think she'll be ok. She was hurt pretty badly, but she's not in any immediate danger. The doctors think she'll be able to fly back to the States in maybe a few weeks. My mom's over there now. We're all pretty shaken."

James was speechless. It was no wonder she hadn't returned his phone call.

"What happened? Oh, she was hit by a car. Yes, it's terrible. She broke a bunch of bones, I think. Me? I'm doing ok, hanging in there, I guess. Yeah, me too, I wish I could see her myself. It was pretty frightening. I mean, we didn't really know how she was until mom got to see her. We were all pretty worried, we still are. I talked to her on the phone, she sounded really tired, but it was really good just to hear her voice. Yeah? No, I'll be ok. There's really nothing for you to do right now. I'm taking care of a few things for her over at the apartment. You sounded sort of worried on the answering machine, so I figured I'd better call you to let you know what happened. Do you have my number? Good. Here's my cell phone number too, in case if you need to get in touch. Ready? Ok, James, I'll talk to you soon."

Lauren was in Paris for a fashion show that weekend. She was supposed to be away for a week. When she left, James offered to drive her to the airport, but Lauren insisted on taking a car service. She didn't want to inconvenience him, she told him.

James was disheartened by Lauren's refusal. He still loved Lauren. He still wanted to be her someone special, someone who drove her to the airport, someone who met her when she returned, someone who welcomed her home with a glad-to-see-you-never-leave-again kiss, someone to spend the rest of her life together with.

Now, he may never see her again. He felt upset, angry, helpless. Tears welled up in his eyes. What could he do? There was nothing he could do. He couldn't abandon his work and fly to Paris. He could only wait, which was sometimes the hardest thing to do. She was alive, and that was a small consolation.

A month passed. It seemed an eternity. The first week was the hardest. James thought of Lauren constantly. He talked to Michelle almost everyday, and she gave him updates that she received from her mom. There was really nothing new each day, but it was reassuring to hear about her, to know that she was still there.

Bit by bit, Michelle relayed to him what she knew of Lauren's injuries. A black eye, a broken arm, a bunch of bruises, a big cut on her scalp. They had to shave off some of her hair to put stitches in. The most serious injury was a fractured pelvis. Her mom didn't mention anything about her needing an operation, but Michelle would ask her the next time she called. And mom said that she had a horrible reaction to some medication and broke out all over her skin. It was pretty serious, the rash even broke out in her mouth and she couldn't eat or drink anything. They had to feed her through an intravenous.

Days wore on, and news of Lauren were more optimistic. She was in less pain. She was finally able to eat a little something. She was able to stand. They took the stitches out. She was able to walk a few steps. She still had a cast on her arm, but the doctors said that she would be able to return home soon, when she was able to walk a little better.

There was no better impetus than coming home for Lauren, and when she heard that she would be able to go home as soon as she walked more steadily, she redoubled her efforts in physical therapy.

About five weeks after her accident, Lauren flew back with her parents to her home outside Philadelphia. James wanted to race down to see her as soon as she came back, but he thought that it was better to give her and her family some time alone. He called her the day after she got back, just to let her know that he was thinking of her, just to let her know that he was there for her, just to say hello, just to hear her voice. She was glad to hear from him, but she was tired. She assured him that she was fine and told him to call back the next day.

Lauren was sleeping the next day he called, so James didn't get to speak to her. Instead, James spent a long time talking with Mrs. Corvo. She was heartbroken and exhausted by the ordeal. She needed to talk to someone herself, someone to share her hopes and her fears, someone to open up to. She needed someone with whom she could speak with candidly. It was not possible to have such discussions with her immediate family; they were too closely involved. She needed someone distant, but not a complete stranger. James was the perfect person. Mrs. Corvo knew him. Mrs. Corvo liked him. She trusted Lauren with him, and he called at the right time.

"James, I don't know what's going to happen," said Mrs. Corvo, "I don't know what we're going to do."

Mrs. Corvo usually received the same response from well-wishers when she spoke about Lauren's accident. She'll be all right, don't worry, things will work out fine. As sympathetic as everyone tried to be, such confident prognostications were not reassuring to Mrs. Corvo. Her daughter laid suffering in front of her eyes. The life that she led was lost. At times, it seemed improbable that Lauren would ever recover, as much as she had hoped and prayed for her daughter.

"Lauren is a strong person. She will make the best of it, no matter what. It's impossible for us to see how things will turn out. It is going to be difficult, but you have to wait for time to go by, then we'll see how things will settle out. You've done everything possible. You can't ask anymore of yourself. You have to get some rest too, for your mind as well as your body …"

Those few words were comforting to Mrs. Corvo. Of course James was right.

Mrs. Corvo and James spoke for several hours. Mrs. Corvo talked most of the time, and James listened to her faithfully. She felt a little better after talking to James. Her mind was still doubtful and preoccupied, but the light of hope and the promise of time helped ease her soul.

Lauren was awake when he called the next day.

"Hey, stranger, how are you?" she asked.

"I'm so-so, how are you doing?" he answered.

"Oh, as well as one can expect, I suppose. It's good to be home, though, I have to say. They were very nice to me over there, but it's good to be out of the hospital."

"Are you eating and sleeping ok?" James asked her a few questions about her health. She lied to him a little, not wanting him to worry, wanting him to think that she was better than she was.

"Thank you for the flowers, by the way, they were beautiful."

James sent an arrangement of pink roses, her favorite. Pink was for friendship, she said.

James drove down to see Lauren on Sunday because he had to work on Saturday. It would have been easy to feel anxious or fearful about the visit during the ninety minute drive, but such distressing thoughts were far from his mind. A single predominant feeling occupied his thoughts. He missed her terribly and he was eager to see her again. It had been almost two months since they had seen each other, and he missed her in a way that he had never felt before. It almost seemed as if a part of his life was missing, and now he had a chance to get it back.

As James drove up to the familiar house, he was overcome with the feeling of how different things were.

Mrs. Corvo answered the door.

"Hi, James, it's so good to see you. I'm so glad that you've come."

Mrs. Corvo gave James a warm hug, a greeting that she rarely bestowed on anyone.

"Lauren was sleeping in her room, let me go check on her."

Lauren slept much of the time after returning home. She was frequently tired. She tried to stay awake that afternoon, expecting James' visit, but she became too weary and drifted off. She was awake when her mother came to her room. The doorbell had roused her.

"Is it James?" Lauren asked.

"Yes, it's James."

How glad she was to hear those words. "Ask him to come up," she said.

Mrs. Corvo returned downstairs and found James sitting expectantly where she had left him. "She's awake. She's waiting in her room."

James knew his way to Lauren's bedroom. He walked upstairs quietly.

"Lauren?" he said softly as he looked for her in the dimly lit room.

"James?" she answered.

It was an emotional meeting for the two friends. He approached her bed and sat down next to the familiar figure sitting there, smiling weakly. Without a word, they reached out and held each other tightly, tears welling up in their faces. These were not tears for sorrow. They were happy, happy to be reunited with each other.

"I'm so glad to see you," said Lauren, wiping off her tears with her hand. "Look at me, I must look a mess." She didn't have a chance to clean up a little before James came up, but it didn't matter. She really wanted to see him. She knew it wouldn't make any difference to him.

James looked at her. She had lost a lot of weight after the accident. She hadn't been sleeping or eating so well, judging from her eyes. There were faint traces of bruises on her face. Her skin was pretty scratched up from the drug reaction, he hoped for her sake there wouldn't be any scarring. That would be devastating to her. She's probably having more pain than she had admitted to. She was getting better physically, but how was she handling things inside?

"You look beautiful to me," answered James, "a little beaten up, but still beautiful." He meant every word of it.

Lauren would have never thought it possible to feel beautiful in the state she was in, but she felt beautiful then. She did not understand it at the time, but she would always be beautiful in his eyes.

The first conversation after a long absence often could be awkward, especially given all that they had gone through. It was natural to be hesitant in talking about the accident. James might be reluctant to have Lauren relive the awful event. Lauren might not want to burden James with the unpleasant particulars. Indeed, close friends might be too sensitive and protective of each other's feelings to bring up such a subject, but James and Lauren were more than just close friends.

They began with innocent topics. She asked him about the drive, whether anything interesting happened at work, things small and trivial. Slowly, they began to talk about the accident. She asked him about how he found out about the accident, what Michelle had told him. He asked her about her hospital stay in Paris, the flight back to the States, how her parents were handling things. Lauren told James the details of the accident. It happened so quickly, everything that followed. It was not difficult for Lauren to tell her story to James. On the contrary, it felt good to talk about it with James.

As James was telling her about his conversation with her mom, Lauren became silent, then a smile rose from her lips. She scrutinized James' face for a moment. An amused expression came over her face, her smile widened and she looked away for a second. James knew that look well, the slight arch in her eyebrow, the knowing smile, the amused look on her face. She was musing over something in her mind, something about him.

James broke off from what he was saying.

"Okay, what is it?" he asked her.

Lauren paused momentarily. "I was thinking that you probably tried to come to Paris."

She was right. He tried.

"I did. I tried, but I couldn't get my shifts covered at work. I really tried."

She knew he did. That was what made her smile. It was the first time she had smiled in a long while.

"I wanted to see you in person, I wanted to see that you were all right. Not that I could have done anything."

"That's not true, it means a lot to me. I'm glad you wanted to come," she said.

It was not so easy for Lauren to get around on her own then. She was still having pain from the pelvic fracture. She walked with a cane and she had to wear a brace on her leg. Lauren wanted to stretch her legs a little bit and go to the bathroom. James helped her off the bed and put on her slippers. He helped her down the hall and waited for her as she shuffled around in the bathroom. Lauren wanted to go downstairs and she leaned on James as they gingerly made their way together.

James helped Lauren to the sofa and they sat down next to each other. Lauren noticed an unfamiliar piece of tupperware that was sitting on the coffee table.

"I made some rice krispie treats for you," said James.

"I love rice krispie treats." He knew that, she remembered. She opened the plastic container and inspected the treats with a smile.

"Ooh, chocolate chips!" She liked chocolate chips in her rice krispie treats. He remembered that, too.

"I'll split one with you," she said to James. Lauren grabbed a couple of napkins and broke one of the rice krispie treats into two, handing James half of the crunchy treat. They took a bite together.

"They're kind of sweet," remarked Lauren.

"Uh, a little too sweet. I guessed I added too many marshmallows."

She laughed as they took another bite of the rice krispie treats.

"You were never much of a dessert guy," Lauren recalled.

"You may not want to finish these," said James.

"Well, at least I can save them as a keepsake."

It was late evening already. Daylight was fleeting during this time of the year, the winter days dispersed quickly into darkness. Mrs. Corvo came into the living room and asked James to stay for dinner. She was loathe to interrupt them. She pulled her husband aside earlier and made sure that Lauren and James would be left alone. She knew that it would be good for Lauren to spend some time alone with James. She felt a little more encouraged after talking to James, and she felt that he would do the same with Lauren, maybe even more so. Her expectations proved correct. Lauren felt better just being with James, talking with him, seeing that he cared for her. She didn't need any inspirational speeches or rallying cries. She wanted kind words and tender thoughts, the soothing airs that James always provided, the compassionate touches which were always a part of him.

Her parents quietly noted that Lauren was more cheerful at dinner than they had seen her recently. She joked with James, and her appetite seemed to be better. Her father was tentative at first, not knowing James as well, not knowing what their relationship was, not knowing what his intentions were; he was not sure of what to say. When he saw the effect that James had on his daughter, he became less wary of him, and he spoke to James in a friendly manner. Mrs. Corvo was delighted, of course, that the sullen mood that had pervaded the house was vanquished for at least one evening.

Lauren wanted to talk to James some more after dinner, and asked him to help her upstairs. They watched a little television, and talked some more. It was approaching midnight before either of them noticed the time.

"I can't believe it's so late. I'm usually so tired by nine o'clock that I go to bed so early."

"Yeah, I think I better get going," James said.

Lauren wanted to see James to the door, but he insisted against it, not wanting her to make the inconvenient effort of going downstairs and back up again. They could say their goodnights there in her bedroom.

"I'm glad you've come," her eyes were misty as she held James' hand.

"So am I." He embraced her tightly, then he kissed her softly on her cheek. The gentle kiss aroused a wave of pleasure over Lauren. Her hands tightened around his warm body as he kissed her. His kiss was warm and comforting, much like himself.

"Goodnight," said James, as they untangled themselves.

"Goodnight," she answered. To herself, she said "Goodnight, I love you." She heard James speaking to her mother downstairs before leaving. She watched him walk out to his car from her window. He looked back for her window and saw her watching him. He smiled and waved back. She returned his smile before watching him drive off. She stayed up for a few minutes before falling asleep. She thought about James, about the accident, about the future. Was he still in love with her? Was it possible? It was a happy prospect, and it was a wonderful dream to fall asleep to.

It was about two in the morning when James got home. He woke up five hours later to go to work. He thought that he would be tired at work after the visit, the driving, the late hours, but he was happy and energetic. Perhaps he was tired, but he didn't feel it. He had seen Lauren. She was okay. She was happy to see him. They were happy together. Perhaps he could dream once again.

Lauren didn't mention anything of it to James, but Brian came to see her the day before, on Saturday. Michelle called all of Lauren's close friends after the accident. She didn't know that things had ended badly between Brian and Lauren. She didn't know that Lauren did not want to see Brian anymore.

To his credit, Brian was genuinely saddened by the news when Michelle called him. He asked Michelle if he could help in anyway, if there was anything he could do. She thanked him for his offer and promised to call him back with more news. Brian asked Michelle to let him know when Lauren got back, he wanted to pay her a visit when she returned.

Brian didn't know what to expect himself in seeing Lauren. There were the few months when they spent a lot of time together, but she was still pretty upset with him the last time they saw each other. He felt conflicted. He thought that he was wasting his time with Lauren. He was getting nowhere with her, she was a tease; but there was a little part of him which believed that Lauren was something special, and that there was hope yet. It was that little part of him which made him want to see Lauren, to try to win her back again.

He had never been to the Corvos' home before, and he got a little lost with the directions he had gotten from Michelle. He misread his own handwriting. He was frustrated when he was lost. He asked himself what he was doing there, why he was doing this. He had better things to do on a Saturday afternoon, he said to himself.

He found his way to the house after the minor mishap. Mrs. Corvo answered the door.

"Brian? It's so nice to meet you. Oh, these flowers are lovely." Brian brought a bouquet of red roses for Lauren.

Mrs. Corvo went upstairs to tell Lauren that Brian was here. He waited in the living room; uncomfortable, anxious, dreading. Mrs. Corvo returned shortly.

"She'd be down in a second," she said.

Brian felt awkward talking to Mrs. Corvo. They had very little to say to each other before he heard her steps descending the staircase. He watched Lauren limp into the living room.

Brian was shocked by her appearance, and his facial reaction reflected his dismay. She looked terrible. He could barely recognize her. She looked nothing like the beautiful creature that had so enraptured him only a short time ago. Her hair was ragged. He could still see where they had shaved her hair to put in the stitches, the scar was still visible. She had bruises everywhere, and she was struggling just to walk a few steps. Worst of all, her face was scarred badly, disfigured by the drug rash. He was horrified by her appearance.

Lauren greeted him weakly, and he gave her a restrained hug. Mrs. Corvo left them alone to talk.

Brian was right, there was nothing there for him. His relationship with Lauren came about because of a mutual attraction, and now that it was gone, they didn't have the passionate friendship that was necessary to keep them together. He was relieved that he had broken up with her. It wasn't necessary to spend any more time with her. He didn't feel obligated to be there for her. He paid his visit politely, asked her how she was, asked her if there was anything he could do, but he was watching the time pass by slowly, determined to leave after an hour's visit.

Brian said his goodbye after the hour and left, saying he had to get back home for something. Lauren would never see him again.

It was a difficult adjustment for Lauren. She went from being young, carefree, healthy, to being badly injured, unable to go anywhere, dependent on other people.

At first, she was concentrating on getting better so she could get out of the hospital, so she could get back home. She was hurt so badly in the accident that she didn't really think much about the consequences of her injuries. When she got the drug reaction, she looked at it as another setback that kept her from going home. The bad part was that the sores in her mouth kept her from eating anything, and it made her weaker.

She finally had time to take in all that happened when she got home. She was concerned about her future. At first, she only wondered what would become of the physical injuries. Once her hair grows back, the scar in her scalp would probably be hidden. The bruising on her cheek and her body were almost gone. She became more concerned about the marks from the drug reaction. The scars were still visible even though the sores were healing slowly. Were they going to go away, or would she have these blemishes forever?

It was frustrating not to be able to do everyday things easily. Her arm still felt funny after the cast was taken off, but at least she could use it again, although she didn't have the dexterity that she had before. She needed help just getting out of bed sometimes. Lauren still had difficulty walking because of her pelvic fracture. Stairs were never much of an obstacle before, now they required a herculean effort. Would I be able to drive again? she wondered.

Lauren began to go to physical therapy. At first, she looked forward to it. It got her out of the house, it made her become part of society again. She saw it as a necessary step in her desire to regain her independence. She would have therapy for a few months, then she would be back to normal again, she wished.

It turned out not to be so simple. She felt out of place at physical therapy. Most of the patients there were much older, recovering from strokes, surgeries, and the like. There was only one patient there who was her age. He was autistic, so she couldn't really relate to him either.

Therapy was not as easy as Lauren had thought. It proved much more difficult to get her body to do what she wanted. The most disappointing part of all was the uncertainty, that she didn't know whether she would ever get better again. Her skin was healing, but she still may have a permanent disability. She would still lose her balance sometimes walking or doing her exercises and fall. The fall didn't hurt as much as the fact that she still couldn't do everything on her own. She hated to be like that, to be dependent on other people.

Lauren noticed that even the subtle things in life were turned upside down. She still attracted people's attention when she went out in public, but it was a different type of reaction she got. Lauren was accustomed to being admired, to be looked at by strangers, it was her career. Now, she was stared at by passers-by because of her accident. She could see the alteration in the faces of the people who looked at her. They no longer admired her. They watched her with curiosity. She wondered what went through their minds as they looked at her. Did they wonder what happened to her? Were they horrified by the scars on her face? Did they pity her? What did they see?

Of all her friends, only Andrea, Peter, and James visited her regularly. It was easy for Andrea and Peter to see her, they came down and stayed with Andrea's parents when they visited her. James, on the other hand, usually drove back late at night after he came to see her.

James tried to spend as much time as possible with Lauren. He even came down and drove her to her therapy sessions sometimes. He would help her with her exercises, supporting her, remarking on her progress, cheering her on. It was good to have James around. She could tell him how she was worried about her scars, how she detested the loss of her independence, how depressed she felt about the whole accident at times. For Lauren, it was easy to tell James all these things. He listened to her. He consoled her. He made things not so gloomy. It seemed like he was the only one who could cheer her up. He could always bring a smile to her face. Things never seemed as melancholy when he was around.

Lauren particularly looked forward to the weekends when Andrea, Peter, and James all came down. By then, she was able to impose on James to stay over at her parents', "so that you get to spend the entire weekend with me," she insisted. James was glad to take advantage of the Corvos' hospitality, the long drives back and forth were tiresome. Besides, he was there so often that they already considered him as part of the family.

One of the favorite things that Lauren liked to do during her convalescence was to play board games with her friends and family. *Trivial Pursuit, Taboo, Pictionary*, they played them all. Lauren and James always stuck together as a team. James had an amazing knowledge of trivia, so Lauren always liked to play on his team, and they were just as good together playing *Taboo*. However, they were most amazing when they teamed up for *Pictionary*. Andrea, Peter, and Michelle were often astonished at their ability to interpret each other's drawings. They were either cheating or telepathic, said Michelle.

Once, the clue was *Ottawa*. James quickly drew a map of Canada and put a star on the country.

"Oh! Oh! The capital of Canada, what is it?" Lauren understood the clue right away, but she couldn't come up with the name of the city. "Montreal? Toronto? Vancouver?" She gesticulated wildly with her hands, then she started laughing uncontrollably. "This is killing me! It's on the tip of tongue!"

James laughed along at her excitement, then he had an idea. He drew a little animal with flippers.

"Oh! I got it! Ottawa!"

Andrea and Peter looked at each other in amazement. "How did you get Ottawa from that? What the heck did you draw? Is that supposed to be a seal?" Andrea asked.

"No, see, that's an otter," Lauren corrected her. "Get it? Otter-wa!"

"Unbelievable," Peter said. "I can't believe you guys got that."

Lauren and James were quite delighted with each other. They laughed gleefully and gave each other high-fives. It became one of those moments that they would forever treasure together.

Lauren and James made plans for her to stay with him for a weekend. It would be like a mini-vacation, she said. Lauren had not been out of the house much since she returned home. In fact, her social life revolved around James, Andrea, and Peter. She had not spent so much time at home with her parents since she was a teenager. It wasn't that she didn't want to be with her family. She appreciated all that her parents did for her. She was grateful for all the time that her sister spent with her. She knew that Michelle had better things to do on a Saturday night than to stay home with her sister. She loved her family, but it would be nice to go away for a few days. It would be nice to have a change of scenery. It would be a small step back to everyday life.

James came down and picked her up on Friday afternoon. It was a beautiful spring day. The skies were sunny and the day was warm. Lauren was in good spirits. She was chatty the entire time during their drive. James was happy to see her so full of energy.

Lauren was glad to see James' place again. It was so familiar to her, the touch, the feel, the warm scent. It brought back pleasant memories. It felt like … *her* home.

James carried her bags to the spare bedroom and went to change for dinner. Lauren plopped down on the sofa and looked around her. Really, not much had changed. She picked up a photo album and leafed through it. There were several pictures of James hiking along canyon trails. It looked like he was somewhere in the Southwest, there was a backdrop of red sandstone formations. It must have been from a trip he had taken before he met her, she thought. She flipped through the pages, casually glancing over the photographs. Suddenly, she came upon some pictures that were familiar to her; pictures of James, pictures of her, pictures of the two of them together. She had seen these photographs before, but they seemed new to her. There were pictures of them at a museum. It was the Museum of Art, she recalled; they went to see an Andrew Wyeth exhibition. There were pictures from their bike ride along the parkway, the two of them at a party, James cooking in her old apartment, pictures of them in a park. Yes, that was the day that they went on a picnic. There was a photo of them taken at an arm's length, their faces were squished together, smiling cheesily for the camera. It impressed her how happy she looked in that picture. Her face expressed a feeling of perfect peace and contentment. It seemed to her that she never looked that way in any other of the thousands of photographs that had been taken of her.

The next photograph was a shot of the two of them walking in the woods. James set up the camera on a tripod to take this picture, she remembered. He thought that it would make a nice photo. They were holding hands, walking away from the camera, surrounded by red and golden leaves, backlit by the autumn sunshine. She thought it was the most romantic picture when she saw it for the first time, and the same intense feelings came flooding back as she gazed at the picture again. She cherished that photograph; she had it enlarged and framed for her. She kept it at her bedside. She woke up to that picture every morning, that is, until she broke up with James. It became too much of a reminder then, and she stowed it away in her closet. It was out of the question to throw it away.

Lauren flipped the page. She knew what the next photograph would be. She could see the image in her mind, a poignant reminder of an impossibly happy time in her life. There it was. The same park, the same path. It was a picture of a kiss. It was her picture. She had an idea for a romantic picture of her own. She held James' face in her hands as she kissed him tenderly. She could remember exactly how she felt, what it was like; the warmth of his skin, the softness of his lips, the fluttering in her heart as she kissed him. She didn't let go of him after the shutter went off and the photograph was taken, she remembered, she continued holding him in her hands, kissing his soft lips. How I loved him, she said to herself.

Lauren put the photo album away when James came out of his bedroom. She asked him where they were going for dinner, James had told her that he made reservations for the evening. "I've been to this place a couple of times," he answered, "I'm sure you'll like it." Lauren changed out of the T-shirt and jeans that she had traveled in and put on a sundress. James was awestruck when he saw her. She was lovelier than he had ever seen her. It was a wonderful change from a few months ago. Her skin had healed completely and regained its natural radiance. The dress fit her beautifully; she had gained back the weight that she lost and no longer looked emaciated. The youthful body that had graced so many photographs and captured so many hearts was once more its old self. Perhaps loveliest of all was the smile that she wore on her face. She was happy, and that made her beautiful more than anything else in the world.

James and Lauren caught a taxi outside his apartment. The address of the restaurant seemed vaguely familiar to her. As the taxi wound its way around the city, the streets became more familiar. Lauren realized where they were going. The cafe.

When she stepped off into the cobblestone street, the cafe was there, as it had always been. She smiled appreciatively at James. It was a great choice. It brought back some good memories.

This time, it was no accident that they were together. They even got the same waitress, Mimi. She didn't recognize them, but they remembered her well. Unbeknownst to her, she had become a part of their past, a part of their lives that they cherished.

"What did we have that first time?" Lauren asked.

"A vege burger and noodles. And cheesecake, I think."

"Yes, and sweet potato fries." That was a wonderful afternoon. It seemed so long ago. "Should we order the same thing again?" she asked.

"I'm game if you are."

"No slurping this time." She remembered.

"I'll try my best, no promises."

James and Lauren shared a bottle of Chardonnay. Lauren offered a toast.

"To good friends."

"To good friends," James echoed the sentiment.

The next day, they took a nice walk around the park. Lauren still had a little bit of a limp when she walked, but she didn't need to wear a brace anymore. They had brunch at a brasserie near the park. In the afternoon they went to a nearby museum.

Lauren was a little tired when they got back to his apartment. She took off her shoes and laid on the couch, stretching her feet.

"Ooh, I'm beat," she said. "We did a lot of walking today."

James lifted her feet and sat down on the sofa next to Lauren. He placed her feet in his lap, took off her socks, and gave her a foot massage. Lauren loved his massages, he had done this many times before when they were together.

"Ohhh, that feels soooo good," she moaned.

After James released the stress in her legs, Lauren asked James if he could do her back. She turned over on the couch and laid on her stomach. James repositioned himself beside her, kneading her sore muscles, soothing away her tension.

She missed his backrubs. They were wonderful. He was wonderful.

Lauren was quiet as James massaged her, then a question came into her head.

"James?"

"Yes?"

"Why are you so nice to me?"
He answered without hesitation.
"Because I love you."
She knew, of course she knew.

Lauren was noticeably upbeat after her weekend with James. Their time together rekindled a lot of feelings that she thought were gone. When she looked inside herself, she realized that the feelings were always there. She still cared for him, even after she had broken up with him. She missed him miserably when they were separated. She looked forward to seeing him more than anyone else after the accident. He was the one person that she could always talk to. He was, in many ways, her knight in shining armor. He still loved her, he said as much. The weekend reminded her of the wonderful time when they were together, how important he had been to her, and how dearly she had loved him.

She still loved him.

Love made all problems small and insignificant. It didn't matter that she hadn't fully recovered from the accident. It didn't matter that she still had a limp. It didn't matter that she still needed help doing things sometimes. She was getting better. She was walking better. The limp was barely noticeable when she wasn't fatigued. She liked having James help her around. She liked being with him.

Lauren had lost much of her confidence in herself after the accident. She took it for granted that she would always be admired, there would always be someone who wanted her, there would always be someone who loved her, and up until the accident, there was no reason for her to believe otherwise. She did not see the possibility of being disfigured by an accident. She did not think that there could come a time when her appearance would elicit feelings of pity rather than feelings of adulation.

It hit her hard to see Brian's reaction. It was clear that he was disheartened by her appearance. She didn't mind so much that he didn't love her, she never thought that he loved her. It was much more bothersome to see that he no longer found her attractive. Her beauty, the one thing that she thought she could always count on, was gone.

She didn't believe James entirely when he told her that she was still beautiful when he first visited her. He was only being nice, he was only trying to cheer her up. As the days went by, as they spent more and more time together, his sincere sentiment began to sink into her, and she slowly began to believe in herself again. She slowly regained the feeling that she was pretty, she was desirable, she would be loved.

Hearing his declaration of love, despite the fact that she broke his heart once, after having gone through all those tough times together, gave her a sense of renewed hope. Life would be happy again. She would be happy again.

A few weeks later, Lauren moved back to the city to finish school.

She took an apartment that was only a few blocks away from James. It was practical, she told herself, to be near him. It would be more convenient when she needed him. Her parents were worried about her being on her own again, but they were somewhat consoled by the fact that James would be near her. They had become very close with James in the past few months. They had faith in him, they relied on him, and they trusted their daughter in his hands.

The transition was not as difficult as everyone imagined. Lauren was well enough to get around on her own without becoming exhausted by the effort. The new apartment was an easy train ride to the university and back. Her classes actually seemed less daunting. She forgot that before, she was working a full time job with odd hours while she was in school. She wasn't encumbered by her career anymore, and she had much more time for studying, much more time for relaxing, so everything was easier.

Lauren had more than enough money to live on, she didn't need to go back to school. She had saved most of her earnings while she was modeling. She thought about retiring, spending the rest of her life watching television, "puttering around", as she imagined it. At the time, it seemed that she really didn't have too much to look forward to in life. There wasn't anything that she needed to do, that she was going to do, that she wanted to do. All of the things that she assumed she would be doing in life, like falling in love, raising a family, riding into the sunset, seemed so impossible to her then.

How things have changed. She was well. She was beautiful. Life was possible once again. So was love.

James wasn't sure what Lauren had in mind for the two of them. If she still wanted to be just friends, he was fine with that. He liked her, he loved her, he was willing to abide by her wishes, even though every fiber of his being yearned to be with her. They had not spoken about their relationship in all of the time they spent together after the accident. He was okay with being friends, he told himself, but deep inside, he hoped for much more.

James helped Lauren unpack her things when she moved back. Books, clothes, dishes, they slowly made their way through her boxes. Most of her personal things were familiar to him, he remembered them from her old apartment. He asked Lauren where to put everything, even though he already had a good idea of where everything belonged. They had unpacked most of the essentials when he came across the picture of them walking in the woods. Just like Lauren, the picture had a special place in his memory. He remembered that day well, he remembered the kiss that followed. James remembered that she had kept the picture by her bedside so she could see it everyday. The picture evoked a bittersweet feeling, it was happy and sad at the same time. He stared at it for a little while, and then he put it back in the box, not sure if it still occupied the same place in her heart.

There were only a few boxes left when Lauren suggested that they take a break for the day. The apartment was taking shape. Although the layout was different from her old apartment, everything was where it was before. Lauren and James took a walk around the new apartment, inspecting it before they headed out to his place. While they were in her bedroom, James noticed that the picture was placed in its familiar place on her bedside table.

Lauren and James walked back to his place to clean up and shower. She was going to stay with him until she got her apartment together. James carried her small overnight bag with him. He still had a lot of her belongings in his apartment; makeup, clothes, books, all sorts of things. Her favorite coffee mug, the one with a frog, was still in his kitchen cupboard. She had never come to get it after they broke up. Her personal things were difficult reminders for him when he came across them at times, but he had kept everything in their places, doubtlessly hoping that she would come back to them.

Lauren and James took turns showering in his apartment; Lauren going first as usual. She was resting on the sofa when he came out of his room, in a clean T-shirt and jeans. Lauren was similarly attired, wearing the Glacier Park T-shirt that she wore on her first visit to his place. She was mindlessly flipping through the television, searching for something that suited her mood. She did that when she was tired. Without her prompting, James suggested that they order delivery for dinner. Lauren was all too glad. "That's a great idea, I'm sort of tired," she told him.

James ran a few suggestions by her; Chinese, ribs, Thai. They decided on Japanese, ordering from *Nori*, a place which they had tried before. It was a long while ago, way back when they were becoming close friends, a little before she broke it off with Brian. Of course, neither of them remembered exactly when they had ordered from *Nori* before, although they were both privately trying to recall exactly when this event took place relative to their courtship.

"We ordered from here before," Lauren was the first to speak up over what was on both of their minds.

"Yeah, I think so," ·James answered. It was before they were a couple, he seemed to remember.

"It was a long time ago," Lauren continued, it was before she had broken up with Brian. "It was on dinner and a movie night."

Lauren loved the evening of dinner and a movie when James cooked for her that very first time. It was not a conscious effort at first, but they continued to have these evenings together. James made dinner, and Lauren brought a bottle of wine and a movie. It was not long before they decided to make dinner and a movie a regular feature in their schedules. On some occasions, when it was difficult to get their schedules in sync, they had dinner and a movie night when James worked all day and didn't have time to prepare dinner. Lauren loved their evenings together, and she would rather forego his cooking than miss a chance to see him that week. *Nori* was on the menu one of those nights. The movie was *Only You*.

Tonight, dinner was fried tofu, chicken teriyaki, sashimi, and miso soup for two. *Nori* was always quick with deliveries, so it was not long before Lauren and James sat down to dinner. They ate informally, as they frequently did when they were together. Lauren and James sat cross-legged on the living room sofa, with the food spread out in front of them on an old coffee table, the television turned on. They always shared their meals, James stretched across to snare a piece of tuna with his chopsticks, Lauren reached over him to scoop up a piece of fried tofu. They were as comfortable and familiar with one other as only long-time friends could be. When James slurped his soup absentmindedly, he apologized for his slurping with his usual guilt-ridden smile, and Lauren, for her part, pardoned him with a sweet smile of her own just as predictably.

Lauren and James had worked hard moving and unpacking all day. They had worked up a bit of an appetite, and their dinner was just enough to feel full without feeling that they overate. James removed the take-out cartons and cleaned the coffee table. He heated some water and returned to Lauren with two steaming cups of ginger-peach tea. Lauren loved the smell of the tea, a little spicy, a little fruity, warm and comforting, not unlike James.

They watched a movie on television. It was one of those black and white films that was shown on the public stations from time to time, an oldie but a goodie, so the saying goes. The story followed the life of a man as he traveled from his boyhood to his last days, centering around the tumultuous relationship between him and the female lead character. She treated him badly, it was easy to see, but he could not disentangle himself. His pain and suffering was evident as the story went on, but ultimately he broke free of her spell and found someone who gave him the love that he deserved, a happy ending for a man who went through so much.

Lauren stretched and yawned after the movie ended. She was feeling sleepy. It had been a long day for her.

"I think I'm going to turn in," she said.

"Goodnight then," James turned to her.

"Goodnight." Lauren leaned forward and kissed him, as if it were the most natural thing in the world for her to do. She smiled at him endearingly as she got up from the sofa.

"I love you," she told him, as she disappeared into her bedroom.

James laid awake after he retired to bed. She kissed him. She told him that she loved him. What did she mean? Was it a friendly gesture, or was it something more meaningful? He felt that there was something more to it. It was difficult to say exactly what it was, but there was something in the way that she kissed him. It was in the way that she held his face, a palpable tenderness, as she was wont to do when they were in love. Her breath lingered hesitantly on his lips as the kiss drew to a close, reluctant to break the intimacy. There was something in the way that she looked at him, the soft gleam in her eye, the gentle smile, an earnest look that said as much in silence as in words. There was a sentimentality and a sincerity in the way she said "I loved you" that was not lost on him. It was not one of those casual "I love you" habitually thrown around by affected people. It was thoughtfully intended, it was meant for him.

As well as he knew Lauren, as well as he understood all of her actions and all of her words, James still laid in doubt. Judgment and reason were often clouded by love and fancy, and he wondered if he were sensing feelings that he wished to be there, if he heard and saw things that weren't really there. He knew that he still loved her, and it was his fondest wish for her to love him in return. Perhaps he wanted it so much that his fantasies encroached upon his remembrances of real events.

James frequently slipped into daydreams when he went to bed, before falling asleep. The dreams were always variations of a common theme, a beautiful (the deeper than skin kind of beauty) woman fell in love with him, they were happy, they lived happily ever after. Many women had unknowingly played the lead in his daydreams, but since he had known Lauren, the starring role had been reserved for her only.

Sometimes, James' daydreams crept into his subconscious, and these dreams took centerstage in his mind as he slept. The fantasy was always much more vivid in his dreamstate; the feelings, the love, everything so real. These were the best dreams. Inevitably, when he awakened, he was filled with a sense of peace and love that lasted for a few perfect moments before he realized that it was only a dream. These few precious moments were the happiest in his life. James would stay in these dreams forever if it were only possible.

There was no daydreaming that night. James thought about Lauren, wondering about her feelings, wondering if they were going to get back together again. How should he act in the morning? He wanted to run out for flowers. He wanted to fill her room with roses and lilies and violets, so that the fragrant petals would be there to greet her when she opened her eyes in the morning.

He wanted to scream out loud that he loved her. He wanted to hold her tight and feel her in his arms again. He wanted to be loved again.

James woke up later than usual the next morning. It was late when he fell asleep, owing to the innumerable thoughts that weighed upon him last night. The day was brighter than usual when he opened his eyes. He looked at the clock radio, it was past nine. He had forgotten to set the alarm last night. He was still lying in bed when Lauren peeked her head into his bedroom. He slept with his door open when Lauren was there, so that she could call him or come in to see him whenever she wanted. He didn't see her standing there. He was still half-asleep, lying prone on the bed, his face flushed against the pillow, eyes closed, tucked underneath the sheets. She watched him for a moment, inspecting the soft outlines of his eyes, the tousled hair, the silhouette of his frame, thinking warm thoughts of him. James, even in his state of lethargy, felt her presence, felt her watching him. He opened his eyes and turned over.

He was greeted by her cheerful smile.

"Morning," he said softly, as he lifted his head with a smile to greet her.

"Good morning, sleepyhead," she answered.

Lauren walked over to James and sat down beside him. Her hair was wet and she smelled of fresh soap. She rubbed his back affectionately as he laid there, thinking of her. The anxieties of what was to come in the morning never appeared in his mind. She was there with him. It was what he needed.

Lauren leaned down and kissed him affectionately on his forehead. He looked at her innocently, warm and secure in her presence. A brief feeling of expectancy flashed through his mind. He felt akin to a stray, wondering if his kind mistress, who had found him and warmed him, would be taking him in. The fleeting idea faded away quickly, he was happy where he was, being with Lauren. He stopped fretting about what was to come, and began to enjoy what was in the present.

Her hand was soft and silky as he held it in his palm. He wondered at the life and the magic that coursed through her body. The touch of her skin was nourishing to him, it provided him with life, it provided him with love. He brought her hand to his lips and he kissed her gently. James turned to see her expression. Lauren was looking at him endearingly, a loving smile on her lips.

"Ready to get up?" she asked him. He nodded silently.

"I'll make some breakfast," Lauren said.

James didn't like having people trouble themselves over him. He wasn't used to having people do things for him. He was much more comfortable in the role of a provider than a recipient, but Lauren was an exception. James liked it when she fawned over him; when she helped him pick out new clothes, when she gave him backrubs, or when she cooked for him. He didn't feel like a burden when she did things for him, he felt beloved.

James got up and showered. Breakfast was ready when he came into the living room. A delicious aroma of fresh coffee percolated through the air. Lauren made scrambled eggs and whole grain toast for him. She made James sit down at the dining table as she served him. Coffee, milk, butter, jam, everything was set at the table. His coffee was just the way he liked it, light and sweet, she remembered.

It was the first time that she had done something for him since the accident. As much as James enjoyed the attention, Lauren was even happier to be useful, to be more of a partner to him. He praised her eggs enthusiastically. Lauren accepted his compliments gratefully, but she realized that he was being excessive. After all, they were only scrambled eggs. Yes, but they were extra special because she made them, he told her.

After breakfast, they walked back to her apartment and finished unpacking Lauren's things. The work took most of the day, with a short lunch break at the Vietnamese restaurant. By late afternoon, most everything was put away. The pictures were hung, the boxes were broken down, stacked with the recyclables, and the two friends began to tidy up the apartment. James cleaned the bedroom and the living room, sweeping away the leftover debris and mopping the hardwood floor to a shine. Lauren organized the kitchen, loaded the dishwasher, and scrubbed the bathroom thoroughly. In no time at all the apartment was fresh and neat, ready to welcome its new tenant to live in.

Lauren went into the kitchen and filled two glasses with soda and ice. She handed James a glass and they sat down on the living room sofa, surveying the apartment.

"Looks pretty good," he remarked.

"Yep. We did a good job."

Lauren turned on the television. They watched old *Bugs Bunny* cartoons while they rested. They laughed and giggled over the cartoons that they've seen hundreds of times before. After the cartoons ended, Lauren flipped over to a nature special on the public station. It was a program on the glaciers of North America. Lauren stretched out on the sofa and laid her head on a throw pillow in his lap. James ran his hands softly along her torso, tracing the lines of her lissome body. Lauren relaxed in his soft caresses. She nestled herself tightly against him. They were quiet and beautiful.

They rested like that together until the nature program ended. They were both feeling a little hungry by then. Lauren insisted that she take him out to dinner, a thank you for helping her move. James relented at her insistence, and she ran in for a quick shower before going out. James listened to the echoes of the waterdrops as he flipped through the channels. He was watching a cooking show when Lauren returned shortly in her terrycloth bathrobe. She sat down beside him on the sofa. He turned his attention to her.

"James, would it be okay if I stayed with you tonight?"

He was caught by surprise. "Yes, sure, that'll be great."

James assumed that Lauren would be staying at her place that night, now that the apartment was ready to live in.

Lauren got dressed and packed a few things into her overnight bag. They went to James' place first, before going to dinner. She dropped off her things and James cleaned up and showered.

She took him to a casual bar-restaurant near where they lived. The menu was southwestern, but the main draws were the margaritas, apple martinis, and Coronas.

They were both hungry. "The hangar steak sounds great. I think I'll get that," said Lauren.

"Ooh, I was going to get that," James said in return. He deferred to her willingly. He got the mesquite ribs instead.

Lauren ordered a pitcher of frozen margaritas. "To the best friend a girl could have," she toasted.

Sometimes it was awful for a woman to label a man as a "friend". This was not one of those times.

Dinner was wonderful. They drank to each other happily. They picked food off each other's plates. Lauren playfully licked the barbecue sauce off James' fingers after he delivered some of his ribs to her plate. They laughed out loud and reminisced freely. It was obvious to the casual observer that they were completely in love with each other. Men were conscious of the affection that James received from the beautiful Lauren. Women were appreciative of the intimacy and friendship that radiated between the two confidants.

Lauren wrapped her arm around James' as they walked back from the restaurant. She felt warm and radiant next to him. She liked holding onto him as they strolled through the streets together. She felt like he belonged to her. He was hers; her friend, her supporter, her partner, her love.

The night was warm. It was Friday, and the sidewalks were dotted with couples walking here and there. They were all in love, to be sure, and each couple probably believed that their love was unique, their love was the most enduring. James and Lauren saw themselves as undisputed rulers among the sea of lovers. Who had a stronger friendship? Who had endured so much together? Who loved as much as they loved?

They drifted back to James' place carelessly. Lauren put her arms around James' neck and studied his sweet face longingly. James held her tenderly against him. She felt happy. Life was perfect. The universe was flawless. She found bliss. She felt almost tearful. She closed her eyes and brought herself to him, reliving the magic of his soft lips.

Lauren and James were back together. Things returned to the way it was before; they exchanged keys to their apartments, they spent all of their free moments together, dividing their time between the two homes. The travel arrangements were much simpler now that they lived so close to one another.

Lauren often went to James' place after her classes. She studied in his living room. He pampered her when she was studying for exams. She often spent the night at his apartment, when she didn't feel like walking back to her place late at night. Slowly but surely, her personal things began to appear in his place, and his things did the same likewise.

There were some changes, to be sure. Lauren and James spent most of their time at his place, not hers. His home became her home. She was there so often that Mrs. Corvo frequently called James' place looking for Lauren, knowing that she was more likely to find her there than at her own apartment.

Lauren, in turn, did more for James. She made dinner for him after his long days at the hospital. She babied him after his overnights, made him breakfast, gave him backrubs, put him to bed. She did the same things for him before, though not as frequently. Lauren came to the realization that previously, she did these things because she wanted to, because it made her feel good; whereas now, she did these things more for his sake, because they made him feel good; and she was happy when he was happy.

Despite the renewal of their affections, Lauren and James did not resume spending their nights together. Lauren used the spare bedroom when she stayed over, and the spare bedroom slowly became Lauren's room. It was as if they felt that it was too soon, that it would be more exquisite to wait, when the time came for them to be together again.

Lauren suggested that they go away for a weekend in the summer. It was a great idea, James agreed, the city could be a bit stifling in the heat. Lauren had some time off in between summer sessions at the university, and James could take some vacation days at work. They could spend the weekend at a country inn, there was a resort on a lake that she heard about, or they could rent a beach-house for the weekend.

The idea of a beachhouse on a summer weekend was too appealing to James and Lauren to pass up.

When Lauren planned their weekend away, she had something special in mind. She wanted to be with James again, she wanted to share her bed with him again. The more time that they spent together, the more she realized how he was such an important part of her life. She saw how much she needed him, how much she missed him, how much she loved him, how much she wanted to be with him.

She decided that she wanted to take a big step in their relationship. She wanted to make love to him. She was ready. He was the one. They had spent so many nights together without crossing that threshold. They had their chances, but nothing ever happened. They were always respectful to each other. It was now time. Lauren had been thinking about this in her mind for a long time. She analyzed all of the potential ups and downs that could surface when they crossed that line. There would be no more nights alone, yearning for James to be there to hold her. The intimacy with James would be amazing and pleasur-able, she saw in her mind, not so awkward and dissatisfying as with her previ-ous lovers. She thought it would make their relationship complete. It would make their love stronger than ever. Besides, recently she had felt the need for physical love take hold deep within her self. It had been a long time since she had made love with someone, and it was almost as if it were a hunger that needed to be satisfied. There were times when she was alone with James when she felt like attacking him and having her way with him right then and there. Perhaps, she thought, it wasn't so much that lovemaking would consummate their relationship, but that lovemaking would make her complete, or rather, her recovery complete. It would make her feel like a woman again, it would make her feel whole again. Lauren analyzed the imagined scenario over and over. She believed that she carefully examined both sides of every aspect, but in reality she only saw the promising perspectives in her mind. Perhaps she wanted to be blind to the potential pitfalls. In her reflections, she always returned to the fact that she loved him, that she longed to be with him. It would be a lovely way to let him know how she felt about him.

Lauren was excited about the weekend and was extraordinarily cheerful. She wanted everything to be special that weekend. She did a bit of shopping to get some pretty new things for herself. She bought a few dresses, some sandals for the beach, and two new bathing suits. It was splendid to be trying on all these new things, to see her healthy body reflecting back at her in the mirror, returned to its once-perfect condition. She had never admired herself so much before, when she was modeling. She took her beauty and her body for granted. Now, she was proud of everything that she saw. She worked hard to get back to her former self, and she was pleased to see the results. She didn't need to hide behind long sleeves and jeans anymore, the scars and the bruises were long gone and she was as flawless as ever.

Lauren felt an urge to show herself off a little. She went to her favorite salon and had everything done, her hair, her nails, a facial, the works. Feeling sexy and beautiful, she stopped at a lingerie boutique that she often passed by. As she wandered among the silks and laces, she found herself wondering what James would like to see on her. Probably something simple, she thought, something silky; he liked silk. It occurred to her that she had never bought something to wear with someone particular in mind before, especially lingerie. It was strange that she was looking at herself through someone else's eyes as she searched for that special something. She settled on a sheer flyaway babydoll with a matching lace thong. It was simple, it was silky, and it was very sexy. James would love to see her in it, she thought.

And, of course, she made an extra stop on the way home, to pick up the necessary protection.

Lauren rented a beachhouse that was located on a quiet seaside near the city. It was already fairly warm that Friday morning as they were leaving, it was going to be a hot weekend. James and Lauren drove out of the city, relieved to be away from the heat.

The beachhouse was a little more than an hour's drive. Lauren and James talked about some medical research that he was doing at work, Michelle's boyfriend, and other little things that popped into their heads. The house was on a barrier island a few miles from the mainland, but there were no connecting roads to the small seaside community. Lauren and James had to take a passenger ferry to get to the beachhouse. They reached the ferry terminal in good time, and it was a nice ride across the bay. The breeze off the bow of the ship, the sunshine reflecting off the water, the lazy clouds drifting across the horizon; everything reflected the expectant mood of the passengers on the ferry.

It was a few minutes' walk from the ferry to their beachhouse. They were in a small hamlet, and everything in the hamlet was a few minutes away from everything else. Without a direct road to the island, there was never much of a crowd there, especially at night as the daytrippers returned home. There were a few small businesses there, a grocery store, a few restaurants, an earthy bar or two. It was quiet, secluded, romantic.

James liked the look of the house from the exterior. It was a small cottage right on the beach. The house seemed like it had stood there for a long time, but it was still in excellent shape. James and Lauren dropped their things off in the living room and looked around the house. The interior was modernized and well-furnished; a fireplace, a brand new kitchen, large screen television, a deck which looked into the ocean. There was even a hot tub out on the porch.

Lauren stepped out onto the deck as James carried their bags upstairs. She looked out into the vast blue waters. She could see the waves form over the near horizon, drifting ashore inevitably, one after another. The water splashed over the sand, washing up in undulating swirls. There were a few bathers walking along the length of the beach. Two children chased each other in and out of the surf, their distant laughter barely perceptible. There was a slight ocean breeze that blew softly inland. The wind was refreshing as it lifted her soft hair, cooling her warm flesh. As she stood there, a sublime feeling of peace and contentment rose inside her, telling her that she was happy, very happy.

There were two bedrooms in the house. James carried Lauren's suitcase to the master bedroom and his bag to the smaller bedroom. He was looking at the view from his bedroom when he heard Lauren's footsteps come up behind him.

"It's nice, isn't it?" he asked her.

"Yes, it's really pretty." She cuddled up softly against his back and looked over his shoulder. Lauren wrapped her hands around his waist, holding him tenderly. Her hair was wonderfully silky against his cheek, her breath warm against his neck. They looked out from the window together.

"James, why don't you bring your things into the other room?" she asked him.

James was pleasantly surprised. He never had a hint of her intention to spend the night together.

At first, he wasn't sure if he heard her right, but he knew he did. James turned around. He was about to ask her if she was sure about this. The look on her face said it all. She was sure.

He took her hands in his and held them gently. She pressed back against his soft fingers tenderly. They continued watching the ocean together, each adrift in their own thoughts. He was happy that she wanted to be with him again. He had waited for her, he was ready to wait even longer. He didn't know if she would ever want to get back together again, although there was nothing that he longed for more in his heart. He felt fortunate to have her back again; he loved her so. He had let her go when she needed him to let go, and now she had returned to him. He was so unhappy when he thought that she was gone from him forever, but that was all over.

All week long, Lauren thought about the weekend. The anticipation was incomparable to the heavenly emotions that now swam about her. She felt as if she were the happiest woman ever. He was the kindest, warmest, sweetest man she had ever known. His love, his friendship, his inner strength had been invaluable to her. She was so happy to be holding him there in her arms. She was happy that everything was coming together for the weekend. She was happy that they would be together again.

They spent the rest of the afternoon lazing around the beachhouse. The day passed by quickly, a few hours spent here and there; lying on the deck, watching the sun roll across the ocean, walking around the narrow village streets; hours that would have been inconsequential and lost in memory if one was not falling in love.

They went to one of the small cafes for dinner. The name of the cafe caught their attention, *Homer's Cups*. Expecting burgers, meatloaf and the like at this quaint little place, they were pleasantly surprised by the menu of grilled salmon, risotto, and "great bread". They shared a plate of grilled vegetables for an appetizer, and the bread did indeed live up to the billing. Lauren loved the apple butter that they served with the bread. James had the grilled salmon and she had the petite filet, or rather, they had the grilled salmon and petite filet. Lauren and James shared their entrees as they always did, delving into each other's plates unapologetically.

Lauren and James were a little tired after their late dinner. They could both see the signs of weariness take hold of each other. James stretched his neck back and forth. Lauren knew that he was tired. Lauren was quiet and slouched a little, the reciprocal gesture that James recognized so well. They walked back to their house in the dark night. There was a half moon rising in the distance. The air was still hot from the day, the balmy ocean breeze which blew between the cottages felt tropical. Their way home was dimly outlined by sparse street-lamps. They cast a romantic shadow on the walkway, a blurry silhouette of two lovers holding hands, two people who belonged to each other.

James, though he was tired, was in a good mood. He scooped up Lauren playfully in his arms as they entered the stone pathway to their beachhouse. She giggled and asked him what he was doing, and told him to put her down, but she loved being carried in his arms. They got the front door opened with great difficulty, but they managed to make it through as James carried Lauren over the threshold. "Welcome home," he said, once they were inside. He kissed her softly on the lips as he let her down from his arms. She returned his kiss as she stood on her own feet.

"Well, aren't you going to carry me upstairs?" Lauren said with a pout.

James smirked, then he grabbed her and tickled her playfully. She let out a scream as he picked her up and threw her over his shoulder. She was laughing heartily as he carried her upstairs. He took her into the bedroom and laid her down gently on the bed. She let herself fall backwards onto the soft mattress, but not before grabbing James by his neck and pulling him down on top of her. They giggled like a couple of kids as they rolled around the bed together. She was on top for a moment, then he was on top, and she again, back and forth they went. Finally, Lauren rolled on top of James and pinned him beneath her. She smiled at him mischievously as she straddled his firm body. James laid calmly beneath her. He didn't try to resist, he was quietly waiting to see what she was going to do. Lauren leaned down and cupped his face in her hands. She held him tenderly as she kissed him forcefully, passionately. It was a kiss with an unmistakable message. The tempestuous yearning that burned inside her had wanted its release for so long. She held nothing back as she sank into him with the full force of her desire.

Lauren had never kissed him like that before. It wasn't that she ever held back, but there was a certain wild, uninhibited abandon in that kiss. He felt as if she were surrendering herself to him.

Lauren laid softly atop James as their sultry kiss lingered on. James returned her kisses delicately, his hands ran across her smooth shoulders, caressing her supple body lovingly. His touch was warm and soothing, like a warm apple brandy. She was wonderfully intoxicated by her lover, melting in his caresses.

Lauren straightened herself as she sat up astride James. There was a tender smile on her face as she focused on his bright eyes.

"Let me go change," she said as she climbed off the bed. She went into the bathroom and changed into her familiar silk pajamas. James listened to the running water as she washed up. He felt happy, as happy as he had ever been in his life. He was in love. They were in love. It was a delicious sensation. It felt like it would never end, it felt like it could not end.

Lauren emerged freshly scrubbed, a slight glow in her flawless skin. James thought that he had never seen her so beautiful.

They spent the night holding each other close. They didn't talk much, they were tired. Yet, they were perfectly content as they laid together, sharing the warmth of their bodies. They drifted off to sleep thinking of each other, thinking how wonderful the world was, how wonderful life was.

Lauren was the first to wake up in the morning. She was lying on her side facing James, her right hand draped across his chest. It was nice to wake up next to him, she thought, he was warm and comforting. She traced the outline of his body in the soft morning haze. He was beautiful, every inch of him. She could feel his chest rising when he breathed. Her mind slowly recalled the events of the previous day, and a smile came to her face. She was perfectly happy staying where she laid.

Lauren and James planned to explore some of the island on Saturday. There was a wildlife preserve nearby, accessible by a footpath along the beach. James packed some snacks and drinks into his backpack, and Lauren carried the beachtowels and other accessories.

The sandy beach was speckled with sunbathers when they left the house. James and Lauren were similarly attired; T-shirts, walking shorts, and sandals. They walked down the beach hand in hand, swaying their arms together now and then in display of their lighthearted mood. The sun was in front of them as they made their way eastward toward the preserve. They took their time strolling along the beach, in no hurry to go anywhere in particular. The small houses slowly disappeared behind them and gave way to tall grasses and wild brush. In an hour or so, they reached the wilderness area, announced by a small time-worn sign staked into the sand. There was a small path ahead; remnants of footprints were scattered about, reminders of the few visitors venturing into the undeveloped area.

James and Lauren walked into the preserve, surrounded by the seclusion and the privacy of the grasses. Even with the sounds of the ocean nearby, the atmosphere was quiet and serene. Lauren and James did not come across a single person as they made their way along the path. There were no voices besides their own, it almost seemed like they were in their own little world. The tranquility was occasionally broken by the birds that hid in the bushes, suddenly flying off at the approach of the two strangers.

The path ran parallel to the shoreline, a few hundred yards from the water. There were intermittent side trails along the main path, all running toward the beach. James and Lauren decided to follow one of these side trails. They had walked a few miles, and they were ready to find a spot to rest, perhaps head toward the beach and relax on the sand. The narrow side trail wound its way between two small sand hills, hiding its course from the hikers.

"What do you think?" asked Lauren.

"We can't see where it goes," he answered, but James was as interested as Lauren in exploring the hidden trail.

"Even better," she said.

They turned down the side trail. The path snaked its way through dense brush beyond the sand hills. From there, Lauren and James could see that the path climbed up a bank a little distance ahead, beyond which they couldn't see any further. The ocean waves became louder as they approached the bank. They seemed to be very close to the shoreline.

James and Lauren climbed up on the bank and surveyed the trail ahead. The path led to a secluded cove along the beach. The small inlet was sequestered from the rest of the shoreline by a small rocky cliff which jutted out into the ocean just to their right, effectively cutting off the cove from the rest of the beach. The shoreline edged inward there, forming a shallow bay. High up on the bank, they could see a long stretch of the beach that led back to the village. The waves pranced about the coastline, drifting in and out of the deserted cove.

"Wow," said James.

"It is so beautiful," she echoed.

They walked into the hidden cove. They were alone on the secluded beach. Lauren opened her bag and took out the beach blanket that they'd brought along. James grabbed one end of the blanket and they spread it out smoothly over the sand. They placed various items on the corners of the blanket to keep it from flying about. It was only a beach blanket, but it was pleasing to them that they worked so well together, wordlessly anticipating each other.

Lauren and James unpacked their gear; suntan lotion, a foldable beach umbrella, bottles of water. It was pretty warm, and James stood up and took off his shirt. Lauren gave a wolf-whistle and urged James on. "Take it off! Take it off!" James did his best of a strip tease as he wiggled out of his shorts, revealing his dark swimming trunks. Lauren admired his body, he was in pretty good shape except for a little bit of baby fat around his abdomen, but even the slight bulge was endearing to her. It provided a soft edge to his trim physique. He smiled at her as he plopped himself down beside her and took a drink of water.

James picked up the suntan lotion and began to put it on.

"Here, let me do that," Lauren offered.

She had James lay down on his stomach as she squeezed a generous portion of the lotion into her palm. Lauren spread the slick cream over his back, rubbing it slowly over his firm body; his broad shoulders, his soft back, his muscular legs. James, for his part, was enjoying the attention immensely, as Lauren gave him a little bit of a body massage as she worked the lotion into his soft skin.

"My turn," she said, as she slapped him playfully on his backside.

Lauren stood up to take her turn at a little striptease. She stood with her back to James and slowly removed her shirt, giving him a tantalizing peek at her bare back. She turned her head and smiled at him seductively. Lauren brought two fingers to her lips and blew him a kiss. She lifted her hands high over her head, like a diver, and began to gyrate to some invisible music. She twirled her T-shirt high in the air before throwing it toward James. She wrapped her arms around her back and slid her hands sensually along her body. Lauren turned her head again with the same mischievous smile and winked at him. She undid the buttons of her shorts and shimmied her hips until her shorts fell in a heap at her ankles, revealing the French cut bikini which accented her legs so well. She stepped out of her shorts and kicked them away. Lauren crossed her arms over her chest as she turned around, playing the role of the timid seductress. She walked toward James and gave him her best come-hither look before she unfolded her arms and stood before him.

"Wow," was all that James could say. James had seen her dressed up and dressed down many times before, but he was still stunned by how beautiful she looked sometimes. She was really something else as she stood there posing in front of him.

Lauren received the compliment with a smile. She liked dazzling people with her looks, and she knew that she had knocked James over.

"I guess you like my suit, huh?" she laughed.

"You could be a model," he joked.

It was meant to be funny, but it triggered a small pang inside Lauren. It was a reminder of the life that she lost. She missed it. She was different now. She knew that James didn't mean anything by it, but it was one of those careless remarks that he let escape on occasion that could be so painful.

Lauren let the words pass. She smiled and laid down beside him, asking him to put some sunscreen on her back.

The day at the cove was beautiful. They had a wonderful time together, undisturbed by anyone. It almost seemed that the cove had been reserved for them, it was meant for them, it was created just for them. They threw a frisbee around, they splashed in the ocean to cool off, but they spent most of the day laying on the beach, tenderly appreciating each other.

It could not have been a better day. The evening was settling in when they started back from the preserve. There was something special about the day, something sweet, something magical. They both felt it, it was as palpable as the ocean breeze, the soft sand, the touch of their hands.

James jumped into the shower and cleaned up when they returned to the beachhouse. He made dinner while Lauren was washing up. Spinach salad, stuffed mushrooms, fresh pasta marinara, and a bottle of Lauren's favorite Chardonnay. They had dinner outside on the deck. The sun was setting; the last hues of orange and red flashed across the waves as they made their way ashore. The dusk settled in over the beach as vague silhouettes hurried back to their homes. Slowly, the twinkle of neighboring lights appeared on stage all along the seashore. Now and then, the waft of burning wood floated through the summer evening; perhaps from a bonfire, perhaps from an old stove.

Amidst all this beauty, Lauren and James were mindful only of each other. They spoke softly of each other during dinner. After dessert, Lauren helped James clear the table. James reclined into a large lounge chair on the deck, and Lauren settled herself next to him. They nestled together closely, like two people sheltered against a storm. They watched the remnants of the twilight disappear in the distance as they finished the bottle of wine together.

Soon, it was dark, and the stars began to glimmer all across the sky. Lauren got up and took James' hand.

"Let's go inside."

They returned inside the house. Lauren retrieved a bottle of champagne from the refrigerator and two flutes from the cupboard. She handed James the wine and led him upstairs hand in hand.

Champagne in bed with the one he loved, it was as sweet and wonderful as it sounded. James and Lauren laid in bed kissing, caressing each other.

"Be back in a second," Lauren said as she excused herself.

James listened to Lauren washing in the bathroom, as he always did when he waited for her to come to bed. Her nightly routine was like a familiar melody to him. He could see what she was doing from the gentle echoes escaping through the open door; the soft percussion of Lauren brushing her teeth, the rhythmic splashing of water as she rinsed her face, the tapering silence as she brushed her hair.

Lauren peeked her head out of the bathroom. "Close your eyes," she said.

James didn't know what she had in mind, but he obeyed her and shut his eyes.

Lauren came out and turned off the lights. "Keep your eyes closed," she told him. She lit some candles that she had brought along for the night, infusing the room with a soft flickering light. She edged up onto the bed beside him. She looked at him sweetly as she sat very near him. She thought how beautiful he looked laying there; quiet, happy, warm. She thought how much she loved him.

Lauren bent down and kissed James softly on his lips. He drank in the delicate scent of her soap and the touch of her silky hair on his cheek as she kissed him. He loved those familiar treasures. A smile rose from his lips, matched by a smile on hers.

"You can open your eyes now," she said.

It took a moment for James to adjust to the darkness. Ever so slowly, Lauren's familiar form came into focus. She was beautiful amidst the soft glow of the candles. He looked into her eyes for a long time before he saw that she was wearing the sheer babydoll. She was simply breathtaking.

He understood her intentions immediately.

"You are so beautiful," he told her.

Lauren ran her hand softly across his chest and down to his navel.

"Lauren …" James began to speak.

She answered his unfinished words with another kiss.

He kissed her back eagerly, but he spoke again when their lips parted.

"Lauren, I need to ask you something …"

Lauren was stopped dead in her tracks. She pulled away from him and sat up in the bed. Suddenly the same anxieties came washing over her again. She knew what he was going to say to her. She knew what he was going to ask of her. She was afraid of what she was going to say in return. She hated him when he asked so much of her. Oh James, why can't you just leave things alone?

She looked at him seriously. "What do you want to ask me?"

"Lauren, do you want to be with me?" he asked. "Not just tonight, but—"

"I know what you mean," she cut him off.

She remained silent for a while. James waited discouragingly for her to say something.

"James, why can't we just have this night together? Why do you have to make it so much bigger than it is?" Her voice was trembling, the way it sounded when she was about to break out in tears.

James reached out and held her hand tightly.

"Lauren, I can't stand the thought of making love to you once, twice, or a thousand times if I knew that we weren't going to be together forever. I love you, Lauren, and I want to be with you always. You mean so much to me. I'm willing to do anything for you, you know that, but I need to know that you're in for keeps."

Lauren looked down at the hand that held her. It was so warm, so kind, so gentle, and yet she was uncomfortable with its touch. She drew away from him. He looked at her hurtfully. Lauren turned her eyes from him. She was so conflicted inside. She wanted him, didn't she? For one night, or forever? She wasn't ready to make this commitment, was she? Maybe she was. If not tonight, when? Maybe she was never going to be ready to make such a commitment to anyone. Maybe she was never going to make such a commitment to him. She loved him, didn't she? Then why couldn't she say those few words? Maybe she didn't love him, after all. Maybe he wasn't the one.

One thing was sure, there were more questions than answers. She could go on analyzing the situation for years and still not arrive at a decision. It was a very painful moment for both of them.

"James, I don't know."

If she wasn't sure then, she was never going to be sure. The same thought arose in both of their minds. James felt incredibly sad. He was silent. His heart was shattered.

Lauren desperately wanted to turn back time, to rewind the clock so that she wouldn't have to go through what she was feeling. It ripped her apart. She was angry at James for asking so much for her. She was angry at him for destroying a wonderful weekend. She was upset at herself. She felt as if there was something wrong with her, because she couldn't give herself to him. Everything that had been going so well in her life was suddenly crashing down all around her.

They spent the night in the same bed, but they were never farther apart. James was already out of bed when Lauren awakened. Neither of them slept well. Lauren was fitful all night, turning over constantly, kicking at the sheets. It took James a long time to drift off, and then he woke up every couple of hours, each time reliving those painful minutes over and over. He saw Lauren toss and turn in the bed. He thought about going to the other bedroom, perhaps she would sleep better if she had the bed to herself, but he wanted to stay with her. This might be the last time that they would spend the night together, he wondered.

Lauren found James in the living room, holding a cup of coffee as he stared out into the ocean. He turned around and smiled when he heard her come downstairs. Wordlessly, they both walked toward the kitchen. He laid down his cup and poured her a cup of coffee, milk, one sugar. She took the mug with a gracious smile. "Breakfast?" he asked her, and she answered with a nod as she took a sip of coffee.

James made some scrambled eggs and toasted bagels. They spoke about the trip back over breakfast. There was a strained effort on both their parts to have a normal conversation. Neither of them wanted silence, even though an uncomfortable silence would have been much easier for both of them. There was a concerted effort to keep the conversation going, to keep the conversation light, to talk about easy things, things that would not upset anyone. It was unthinkable to talk about last night.

After breakfast, they took a last walk along the beach together. The weather had cooled down overnight, and it was not as humid as it had been. The beach, the sun, the children playing in the sand, everything was the same as it had been all weekend. They walked for a long time quietly, thinking, reminiscing, regretting. Their house had disappeared from view long ago before they decided to turn back. Lauren offered her hand to James; there was a bittersweet smile on her face. James held her hand gratefully, he brought it to his lips and kissed her slender fingers, then they made their way back, walking hand in hand.

The trip back home was much the same. There was the same strained effort to keep things superficially light. They didn't want to have another disagreement. They didn't want to have anything negative happen this day. If this were to be their last day together as a couple, they didn't want to leave each other with bitter memories.

James dropped Lauren off at her apartment. It remained unsaid, but they both understood that she would not be going home to his place that night. James took out Lauren's bag from the car. She hugged him and kissed him goodnight.

"I'll call you soon, okay?" she said.

"Okay," he said, as he forced a sad smile to his face.

They returned to their respective places. There was no crying that night, just a deep, dull, unrelenting pain in their hearts. It was something they had to get used to.

James and Lauren didn't talk over the next few days, perhaps there was nothing to say. James received a letter from Lauren just before the weekend.

Dear James,

I know you're not expecting a letter from me right now, but I think this letter is long overdue. Everything has been so crazy and so mixed-up for the past few months that sometimes I think I lose focus of everything that is going on. I am so thankful that in some way I have been able to regain a little bit of normalcy and a little bit of routine back in my life. It gives me time to think and to take some account of all the twists and turns that have happened to me.

First of all, I want to tell you that you have been more important to me in these past few months than you could ever imagine. In all honesty, I don't know what would have happened to me if you had not been here for me. You have been a friend, a confidant, a psychoanalyst, a chauffeur, a nurse, and a million other things for me. My words simply could not express that, of all things, I have been more thankful for you than anything or anyone in these hard times.

I have also become attached to you in a way I never thought was possible. You have been a true friend in every sense of the word. In a way, I feel I have become too dependent on you, and I am afraid that it is too much of a good thing. Now that I'm back in school, it has been too difficult not to be able to see you and talk to you every second of every day. I miss you so much that it becomes distracting at times. You have been great, but in a strange way, I feel I have to learn to go on with my life without you. Does that sound crazy? It sounds foolish, I know, but I think you understand what I mean.

You will always mean a lot to me, and I can never thank you enough for all that you have done. I don't know what the future holds for either of us, but I hope that we will always be friends. It would be unbearable to think otherwise. I hope you can understand what I'm trying to say, and that you would not be too upset with me for what I'm asking of you. Even to me what I'm saying seems completely ludicrous at times, but I think it will be the best thing for both of us. I will miss you badly, you know that.

Love, Lauren

James wept on and off all night in his lonesome apartment after reading Lauren's letter. Her meaning was clear. The ominous feelings which surrounded him after the weekend had come to pass. He was right. She didn't want him. She never wanted to be with him. No one wanted to be with him. He was just another frail, uninteresting, useless being who did not deserved to be loved. The self-loathing continued deep into the night.

James was always insecure in the things he believed that a woman looked for in a man. He felt that he wasn't good-looking enough, he wasn't muscular enough, he wasn't rich enough, but he always believed that he had something to offer. He believed that if anything, he was nice, he was kind, he was funny, and that was enough for him to hope to win someone's heart.

Lauren's rejection shook his faith. She knew him well. She had seen his good side, she had seen his bad side. She knew his strengths and his weaknesses. She recognized all that he had to offer, but it wasn't enough to win her heart. Lauren, who knew him to be funny, nice, and kind, and who, in some small way, loved him, could not fall in love with him. She did not want him as her soulmate, she did not want to spend her life with him. It was crushing. Perhaps, he felt, that he did not have so much to offer after all, his heart and his soul were not enough to counterweigh his many weaknesses, he would have to be content to be alone for the rest of his life.

James felt hopeless. There was no reason for him to try any more. There wasn't a single woman out there who wanted him. It would all end in the same way. He was undesirable. He was unlovable. He was nothing. He would never ask another woman out again. There was no point to it, he reasoned to himself, it was hopeless.

Perhaps of all the things he missed about Lauren, James missed the dinners that they had together at home. It was disheartening preparing the meals just for himself, it was a poignant reminder of his loneliness. He missed having Lauren peek over his shoulder as he cut and diced. He missed having Lauren kiss him on the neck as he worked over the stove. He missed sitting down to the table with Lauren. He missed sharing his dessert with her. It was so lonely having dinner by himself.

There were a lot of other things he missed about Lauren. He missed the long talks that they used to have over the phone. He never had such wonderfully engaging conversations like those with anyone else. There was the way that she smiled when she saw him; the sparkle in her eyes, the slight dimple in her cheek. There was a warmth that radiated from that smile, that let him know how happy she was to see him. He missed watching television with her; the way she laid her head in his lap as she stretched out on the sofa, the way that she held his arm when she nestled close to him, the way they looked at each other mistily at the end of a romantic movie. All of these little things were so endearing to him, and they were all gone.

James never felt so forlorn in his life. He had never felt so desperately lonely before he met Lauren, though there was no one in his life then. He did not know the simple pleasures of having someone by his side, someone special to be with, someone intimate to cherish. He did not know what it was like to lose Lauren. It was so nice being with her.

All of that was over.

Lauren found a package waiting for her when she returned home from classes on Monday. Her doorman told her that James had dropped it off after she went to school. She carried the large box to her apartment. James had taped the box carefully, but Lauren knew what was inside. She cut through the packing tape with a pair of scissors and opened the box. It contained her belongings which she had kept in James' place; her makeup, her books, her Glacier T-shirt, her coffee mug, they were all there.

She had not thought of getting her things from his place. She was a little afraid of talking to him. It had been a difficult decision for her. It had been a difficult letter to write. She truly believed that breaking up would be the best for both of them. She knew that it would hurt him. She knew that she hurt him. It would be so difficult to hear the pain in his voice if she spoke to him.

Lauren had planned to call him midweek, after a few days had passed by. She knew that he was working during the day on Thursday, and that he would be at home later that night. She would call him, ask how he was doing, and explain to him why it would be for the best. She was ready to say that she was sorry, she never meant to lead him on, things just never worked out the way they had hoped.

Lauren felt a little sad as she unpacked the box. Every little thing was a reminder of him. It was inevitable that she began to feel doubtful about the course that she had chosen. He was sweet and caring. She loved him. She had never been so close and intimate with anyone. Why did she choose to throw it all away? It was hard to remain resolved to abide by her choice. She had thought things over a thousand times before she wrote the letter. Nothing had changed, nothing really, except his absence.

James seldom, if ever, talked about his personal life with anyone, especially at work. Even though he didn't say anything, his friends at work could sense that there was something amiss about him, manifest in subtle tones. He wasn't his funny self, he wasn't as enthusiastic in teaching the residents, he didn't smile as much, his hellos were not as warm. A few people were worried about him, wondering what was going on. He told everyone that he was okay and nothing was wrong whenever anyone approached him. "Just a little down in the weather, that's all," he would say.

Jessica was the one person at work who had some idea of what was happening. She had become friends with James during her residency, even though he was her teacher and her supervisor. She witnessed the ups and downs of James' relationship with Lauren. She was there when he first fell head over heels for Lauren. There was a motion of suppressed joy in his voice when she asked him why he was so cheerful. She remembered the first time she met Lauren, at the hospital, and how happy she felt for James. She remembered how radiant he became whenever she asked him how things were going with Lauren. She remembered how depressed he got when Lauren broke up with him. It hurt her to see his spirits so despondent. She remembered her surprise and delight when James told her that they were back together a few months later. There was the dinner at the *York Grill*; James and Lauren, Jessica and her husband. That was when she found out about Lauren's accident. She saw that he was in love with her just as ever before. She hoped that Lauren would not break his heart again.

She saw that, once again, James was in a dejected and sullen mood all week. She knew that it probably had something to do with Lauren. She wanted to find out what was happening with him, but she was almost afraid to ask him how things were going with Lauren. Jessica was almost afraid to talk to him at all. She got the same response as everyone else when she asked him how he was, but she knew he was lying, he could barely look at her face as he spoke to her.

A couple of weeks went by, and Jessica saw that James was growing worse. He seldom spoke to anyone at work unless it was absolutely necessary. She practically had to corner him at times to get him to talk to her. There was a look of pain in his face whenever she saw him.

With much effort, Jessica finally convinced James to have dinner with her. She thought that it would be good to get him out, and they could talk in a way that they couldn't talk at work.

"What's going on with you, James?"

"Oh, nothing, just feeling a little blah."

"How are things going with Lauren?" she asked nervously.

"Oh, it's over between us." He was completely crushed, she could see. "She wrote me this letter, saying that we should spend some time apart, that we should just be friends."

Sometimes it was surprising how the word "friend" could have such an ominous meaning.

"Oh, I'm so sorry to hear that."

"Yeah, it happens," he answered. James turned his face away. "I have to step out for a second," his voice was trembling as he got up from the table.

Jessica followed closely behind him. She found him sitting in an alcove a little ways from the restaurant. He was crying. She sat down next to him and put her arm around his shoulder, trying to console him. She didn't say a word, she let his tears flow.

"I'm sorry about this," James said, when he had dried his tears a little.

"Don't be sorry. It's okay."

James didn't want anyone to see him like this. He didn't want anyone to see him so depressed, so vulnerable. He didn't want anyone to feel sorry for him. Still, he was glad that Jessica was there. He was glad that she was there to listen to him. He was glad that he had someone that he could talk to. He was glad that she was there to hold him.

It hurt Jessica to see James so shattered. He was her friend. She knew him to be a kind, caring person, and here he was, completely devastated. She felt for him. She felt that he deserved better. She felt that he deserved happiness. She wished that she could ease his pain somehow, she wished that there was something she could do. She did not feel that she was being helpful at the time, but she was; she was there for him, she was there to listen to him, she was there to hold him.

They skipped dinner and went back to James' place. He was still quite sad, but he wasn't as emotionally charged. Jessica was worried about him, but James assured her that he would be all right. She left him reluctantly and called him when she got home. He sounded a little tired, but much calmer than he was earlier. She said a little prayer for him before she went to bed.

Jessica did everything possible to get James out of his depression, but he had sunk into a melancholy from which it was impossible to surface. James settled down from his emotional rollercoaster, but he was never the same again. He went to work, he came home, that was the extent of his life. He did everything with a mindless automaticity. He never went out socially. Jessica found it impossible to persuade him to go out anymore. She tried to set him up with some of her friends, but he always declined politely. James went on living, but it was a joyless existence.

Lauren and James still talked once in a while. They saw each other every few months, there was still a strong friendship between them. She still cared for him, and he still loved her as much as ever, but now their relationship took on the character more of a tragic unrequited love. Lauren asked him about his work, his life, always hoping that he would not sound so depressed, always hoping that there was someone new in his life, someone who loved him.

James, in his turn, also asked Lauren about the goings-on in her life. He was very happy that she was doing well in her classes, and that she would complete her degree soon. Although he dreaded it, he asked her about her social situation as well, almost because he felt an obligation to do so. Lauren always told him that she wasn't dating anyone, knowing that this was a sensitive topic, not wanting to hurt his feelings. She had a few casual dates that she never mentioned, but eventually she found a serious boyfriend. She had been seeing him for a few months before she reluctantly mentioned him to James. James was wounded inside, but he carried on the conversation, seemingly interested in her new lover. Lauren told him that Ben was a teacher. They met through a mutual friend. He was nice, they had gone on a few dates. James was natural and calm as they spoke about the new boyfriend. He seemed to be fine hearing the news, and he seemed to be genuinely happy for her. He was so convincing that Lauren believed that he really was fine with everything, that he had gotten over her; but he wasn't fine, he was hurt, he was disheartened, he just disguised it well.

The following December, Lauren finished her classes and completed her college degree. The university held a small ceremony for the winter graduates, and she invited James to come see her in her cap and gown. There was to be a small celebration dinner afterwards, and she insisted that James would be staying for the party. It had been just about a year and a half since they had separated, and somewhat to her surprise, she still kept in touch with James. They still spoke to each other every month or so, and they had coffee together once in a while. The two friends updated each other about the happenings in their lives; school, work, ski plans, Ben, and the like. James became resigned to the permanence of Ben. He was not a casual interest, they were very happy together. It still hurt James to hear Lauren talk about Ben. Ben was a great cook (… she used to love my cooking …), what a great time they had in the country last week (… remember our bicycle trip?), how happy she was with Ben (… I remember how she smiled when we were together, how happy we were at the beachhouse before …).

The same emotions and the same self-loathing overcame him every time they spoke, or even when he thought of her every now and then. He wasn't good enough for her. He wasn't good enough for anyone. He had nothing; no looks, no body, no interests, no personality. He had nothing which would attract any woman. He had nothing. He was nothing. There was a terrible pain in his heart every time these thoughts came over him.

James was happy for her success, despite his melancholy. He was proud of her. Lauren was happy to see him at her graduation. She had always believed that she would have never made it without him.

Lauren was beaming as the center of attention that day. There were a lot of familiar people at the dinner; Lauren's parents, Michelle, Andrea and Peter (now married). James was happy to see them again; he had not seen most of them since Lauren and he had broken up. It was nice to catch up with Andrea and Peter. It was nice to talk to Lauren's parents again. Amidst the warm flow of renewed acquaintances, there was one unfamiliar face, Ben.

It was the first time that James met Ben person to person. He had spoken to Ben perfunctorily once or twice before, when Ben answered the phone when he called Lauren. How that hurt him so! James greeted Ben with a warm handshake when Michelle introduced them. They spoke a little about Lauren before the ceremony began, then they sat down and watched the proceedings quietly.

Ben was everything that James imagined. He was perfect. He was very handsome, with thick wavy brown hair, a strong profile, and a deep bass of a voice. He was in great shape, Lauren had told him that he biked a lot. Ben had everything that James thought he himself lacked-looks, strength, money; all those things that he had been always insecure about. And of course, Ben had Lauren. James wasn't sure how he felt about Ben, it was a mixture of envy, self-loathing, and hopelessness. It was trite, he thought to himself, but the Laurens of the world would always be with the Bens of the world, and people like him would always end up with no one to love.

Lauren was glad to see them talking after the ceremony. She was a little worried that it might be awkward, having the two of them together, but the two important men in her life were talking amiably. Lauren was worried that it would hurt James to see her with Ben, but her fears seemed to be allayed. She really wanted James to be there. He was so much a part of her, and she felt that he had as much to do with her graduation as she did.

The small party made its way to the restaurant. Lauren made the rounds and chatted with everyone, but she paid special attention to James, not wanting him to feel neglected, not wanting him to feel alone. She seated him next to her at dinner. They spoke like old friends; easily, warmly, without restraint. She was hesitant to display her affection for Ben in front of James, but she was comforted by his manner, so much so that she was willing to let Ben kiss her in front of James. No one could have known that beneath the pleasantries and the smiles, James was dying inside.

Lauren had a great time at the dinner party. It was the end of a long way back for her, the culmination of a lifetime of work. Physically, it was impossible to tell that she had been in such a terrible accident, that she had almost died. She was proud of herself at finishing her classes, it was something that she had always wanted to do. She had a part-time position lined up, and she would be working again. She had even done a few shoots for her modeling agency, now that she was as beautiful as ever. And of course, she had Ben. He was wonderful and loving and everything else. He may even be the one. Everything was coming together.

James and Lauren spoke about her job over dinner. "So, when are you going to start?"

"I'm actually taking a little time off. I have a couple of months before I start. We're going to go to Hawaii for two weeks."

"Wow, they sounds fun, where will you be going?"

"Maui, Kauai, the big island …"

The party broke up around midnight. Everyone was in high spirits as they said their farewells, promises were made for another get-together. Lauren's parents went home with Michelle, Andrea with Peter, Ben with Lauren; James was the only one to go home by himself. James was in a deep depression as the taxi took him back home. He felt ill.

There was snow on the ground when Lauren returned from Hawaii. The city was swept over by the frosty whiteness, and the streets sat in a subdued stillness. Lauren and Ben were barely home in their apartment when the phone rang. It was Andrea.

"Hey, how was your trip?" she asked.

It was very nice. She had a wonderful time. Ben was sweet and fun and romantic. They couldn't get enough of each other. She loved him. She loved him.

"Can you come over tomorrow?" Andrea asked.

"We're planning on staying in tomorrow to rest up a bit."

"I really need to see you tomorrow," Andrea insisted.

"Sure, I guess I can come out for a little while. What's so important?"

Andrea didn't answer her question. "Come over in the morning, I'll be here." Andrea made Lauren promise to come over. Lauren acquiesced. Lauren was going to ask her again what was so important, but Andrea had already hung up.

Lauren was glad to see Andrea after her trip. She went to kiss her hello on the cheek, but Andrea pulled her in close and embraced her tightly. Lauren could feel Andrea trembling slightly as she embraced her. Lauren looked at Andrea's face and saw that she was visibly distressed; she was very upset about something.

Lauren was suddenly worried. "What's the matter? All you all right? Is Peter okay? What's going on?"

They sat down on the sofa. "I have to tell you something, Lauren …" Andrea trailed off. She looked away from Lauren, hiding her face, she was mustering up the strength to continue.

"What? What is it?" Lauren reached out and held Andrea's hands. Andrea squeezed her hands tightly.

Andrea looked up at Lauren. "James was in an accident while you were away. He's gone."

Lauren turned white. She felt like someone had just stabbed her in the heart.

"What happened?" she stammered.

"We had a big snow storm when you were away. James was trying to drive home when his car got stuck in a snowbank. It looked like he was trying to stay warm in the car, but the exhaust was blocked and he died from the carbon monoxide. It was in the news, that's how I found out. They said he never knew what hit him."

Lauren felt as if she were torn into two. Her mind was a chaotic mess. No, it couldn't be! She began sobbing uncontrollably.

Andrea reached out and held her friend close to her as Lauren cried her heart out.

"I'm really sorry about James," she murmured softly, "I'm sorry about the accident."

Only Lauren knew that it wasn't.

EPILOGUE

It was the first time that Lauren had experienced the death of someone so close to her. She felt eerily calm as she stood over James' tombstone, staring at the earth which held someone that was once, and that was still, so dear to her heart. Her heart was full of sorrow, regret, helplessness. Why, James, why? She knew the answer, but it was too painful to acknowledge. He had helped her escape from her own despair, but he couldn't save himself.

As time wore on, Lauren recovered from the wound. Whether the pain had subsided, or whether she became numb to the pain; she couldn't tell. Her life slowly regained momentum, and she emerged from the shadow of James' death. Ben and she became engaged and they were married a few months later. They had their honeymoon years, then two darling children; everything was wonderful and she couldn't be happier. Every now and then, some little something would recall Lauren to the painful memories that still grasped at her; a man giving up his seat on a bus, a game of *Pictionary*, a glimpse of a sand dune. She kept the secret to herself. She could never share that piece of her heart with anyone, not Andrea, not Michelle, not Ben. It was hers and hers alone. It was a pain that would never go away.

978-0-595-42401-6
0-595-42401-5

Printed in the United States
91050LV00006B/74/A